"No wonder your marriage broke down!"

Elisa's voice held amazement. "You're medieval. What am I supposed to be?"

"All you're required to do is look after my daughter for a fortnight. I don't know why you're making such a drama out of it. I'm not going to chase you at night. Penny's disturbed enough without me introducing loose women into her life."

"I am not a loose woman!" Elisa stormed.

"I'm prepared to take your word for that," Rafe told her coldly, "and you can take my word that you won't be treated as one. It's only if you invite any boyfriends back that you'll find out how much of a bastard I can be."

"I don't believe this," she murmured wonderingly. "You kidnap me, insult me, assault me, do every damn thing to force me into a job I don't want, then behave as if I'm the one on sufferance. You're crazy."

ANNE BEAUMONT started out as a Jill of all writing trades, but she says it was her experience as a magazine fiction editor, buying stories and condensing them for serialization, that taught her to separate the bones of a story from the flesh. In her own writing she starts with her characters—"a heroine I can identify with, then a hero who seems right for her." She says lots of writers work in reverse, plot first, then characters. "That's fine," she says. "If we all had the same method, we might all be writing the same books, and what a crashing bore that would be!" In addition to Anne Beaumont's contemporary romance novels the author has written historicals under the pen name of Rosina Pyatt. She lives on the Isle of Wight, with its beaches and woods, and has three children, of whom she is immensely proud.

ANNE BEAUMONT

that special touch

Harlequin Books

TORONTO • NEW YORK • LONDON
AMSTERDAM • PARIS • SYDNEY • HAMBURG
STOCKHOLM • ATHENS • TOKYO • MILAN

Harlequin Presents first edition January 1990
ISBN 0-373-11231-9

Original hardcover edition published in 1989
by Mills & Boon Limited

CHAPTER ONE

'I'M IN danger,' Rich said, his handsome dark head leaning over hers, throwing her face into shadow, 'of becoming interested in you as a woman—as well as a case history. A little bit of encouragement on your part and...' His voice trailed away suggestively.

He was stretched out on the sand beside her, his long, muscled frame clad in black trousers and white shirt. Without opening her eyes Elisa put one hand against his chest and pushed him gently away. The sun kissed her face again. She stretched lazily on the raffia beach mat and tried to sink into slumber.

'That's not encouragement,' Rich complained, taking her hand from his chest and kissing each finger in turn. 'There's no need to play hard to get. I don't need the old hunter's instinct awakened. In case you haven't noticed, I'm in full cry already. Besides, I prefer a receptive woman. Saves time.' There was no response. His voice deepened. 'What about saving some time, Elisa?'

'Rich, stop being such a pain,' she begged.

He grinned, turned over her hand and kissed the palm. 'I knew you loved me.'

In spite of herself, Elisa opened her eyes and smiled. Rich's sense of the ridiculous was one of the nicest things about him. 'Go and pursue your sociology studies somewhere else,' she scolded him, but without rancour. 'Soon——'

'I'm not pursuing my studies. I'm pursuing you. You can't lie there like some ancient Greek goddess washed up by the waves without expecting a man to lay his heart, hand and all other relevant parts at your feet.'

'Soon,' she continued, as though he hadn't interrupted, 'the holidaymakers will be back in force. The shower's over, the sun's scorching, there'll be customers for you and maybe some for me. In the meantime, let's just laze. We were both up till all hours teaching Greek dancing. You might be used to it, but I'm not. I was only doing a favour. It's not my regular way of earning a living, remember.'

'Greek goddesses don't nag,' Rich told her soulfully. 'They accept adoration as their due.'

'I'm English, weary, and I'll swear at you in a minute,' she warned him pleasantly.

'Elisa! Goddesses don't swear.' He saw her close her eyes in exasperation and changed tack. 'El*ee*sa,' he repeated, stressing the name, savouring it. 'A lovely name. Unusual. Exclusive. Just like you. Er—you wouldn't like to be a little less exclusive, would you?'

Elisa swore. He gave a shout of laughter and she laughed with him. When they'd simmered down, he said, 'I take it you're only interested in being one of my case histories?'

She groaned. 'No, I'm not. I'm only interested in being asleep.'

Undaunted, he began tracing a line down her face, his finger moving lightly from her forehead to her nose, as he said softly, 'You must be interested in being a woman, looking the way you do, and in case you haven't noticed, I'm a man.'

When his finger reached her lips, she bit it.

'Ouch!' Rich's pained expression swiftly turned to a grin. 'That's it, Elisa, my love, you owe me a bite.'

Then they were rolling over and over in the shower-dampened sand, laughing, wrestling, and with Elisa doing a lot of uncharacteristic squealing. Richard, for all his Bachelor of Science degree and the weighty thesis he had come to Corfu to research, was still very much a boy at heart; and Elisa wasn't above forgetting her cares and being a girl.

Rich was on top of Elisa and she was. giggling and fending his mouth away from her neck when a voice, masculine, cold and contemptuous, said, 'Are either of you responsible for service in this café?'

Rich was, as his uniform black trousers and white shirt attested. They both stopped struggling and turned their heads, as though they had been caught out in something naughty. It was the way the voice made them feel.

The café behind them was large, but no more than a patio enclosed by a low whitewashed wall with rough-hewn wooden poles supporting a thatched roof. On the far side was a garden bright with the reds, whites and pinks of geraniums and roses, through which a path meandered to the hotel proper.

Standing a few feet away at the beach entrance to the café, leaning arrogantly against one of the roof supports, was a tall, fair-haired man. Even if he hadn't spoken, Elisa would have known he was English. What was more, he was no run-of-the-mill tripper.

For one thing, he was wearing a lightweight business suit, beautifully and expensively cut, a shirt that fitted so well it had to be handmade, and a discreetly striped tie; for another, he looked as if the Ritz would be more his natural habitat than this free-and-easy package-holiday resort.

What's he doing here? she wondered, while her trained artist's eyes automatically noted his features. His fair hair was cropped close in what looked like a ruthless attempt to reduce curls to crisp natural waves. Golly, he must have looked like Bubbles when he was young, she thought erratically, blinking away a swift mental picture of Sir John Millais' famous painting of the bubble-blowing little boy.

Her gaze moved on, studying the strong, straight nose and the firm, strong chin, separated by a finely moulded mouth that looked as though it didn't know much about smiling. Why did he look so angry? And why was his anger directed at her? It was Rich who was wearing the waiter's uniform!

She met his eyes and blinked again. He had Paul Newman eyes. A lighter, colder blue than her own, with an almost unnerving clarity. Killer's eyes, she had always flippantly called them. But she didn't feel flippant now. She was tingling with a vicarious thrill as she found herself contemplating what an achievement it would be to turn them into lover's eyes.

Then she wondered if the sun was boiling her brain, throwing out fantasies that had nothing to do with the reality of his dispassionate gaze, and it *was* dispassionate now. Whatever anger, for whatever reason, had flared, had since been dismissed. His eyes were looking at, into and through her, as though she had nothing to offer that merited further attention.

She was indignant, justifiably so, but that didn't stop her becoming embarrassingly conscious of Rich astride her scantily clad body. No, not so scantily clad! Her navy blue swimsuit was more of a two-piece than a bikini, chosen more for comfort under shorts and shirt than for maximum exposure to the sun.

A swift downward glance assured her top and bottom were still snugly in place. Nothing had come adrift during the wrestling match. So why did she feel guilty? More to the point, why didn't Rich do something so the man would go away and dissect somebody else with his disapproving blue gaze?

Rich did do something eventually, in his own good time. He eased himself away from Elisa, slapped her thigh affectionately as he stood up, and said, 'You still owe me a bite somewhere.'

Elisa wished he hadn't done that, said that, made it seem—— She checked herself abruptly, angrily. The man could think what he liked and to blazes with him. He had no right to disapprove of her. She wasn't the one who'd kept him waiting for service.

She watched Rich brush the sand from his clothes, saying with his engaging white smile, 'Service, sir? I'll be right with you.'

Only then did Elisa notice the man had a small child with him. She had the same fair hair, long enough to curl wildly about the ribbons that divided it into two neat bunches. Before they both turned back into the café she had a swift impression of wistfulness, perhaps even sadness.

Not surprising, Elisa thought resentfully, if the poor little lamb had that cold fish for a father. She reached for her raffia mat, shook the sand from it and lay down again. After a few minutes she turned over on her stomach. It was no good. Now that she had every opportunity to sleep, she was wide awake.

She knew why. The fair-haired man had disturbed her in more ways than one. She raised her head suspiciously, but he hadn't chosen one of the tables overlooking the beach. She wasn't being observed, although she was becoming crowded. As she'd predicted, the beach was filling up. Soon there would be an endless line of oiled

bodies sun-worshipping along the narrow stretch of sand
that edged the wide sweep of the bay.

Elisa sat up, restoring her equilibrium by drinking in
the beauty of the different blues of the bay, the different
greens of the trees burgeoning in densely packed
splendour on the surrounding hills. An artist's paradise.
Anybody's paradise.

So why had the fair-haired man been so—so miserable?

The question intruded unbidden, unwelcome, but it
had its intriguing aspects. He had made something stir
within her, something she had believed dead. Was it
possible . . . was it *really* possible . . . that she had finally
run far enough, and for long enough, to get over Austyn?
She'd allowed herself a year to work the miracle, dis-
rupting her life, career—everything—and there were still
more than three months to go.

Yet up until now it had seemed so much harder to get
over a love that had never fully flowered than one that
had been indulged. There'd been so many ifs and buts
and might-have-beens to torment her. No sure
knowledge, no certainty about anything, except of course
that she'd done the right thing. For everybody else, that
was.

For herself, she still wasn't convinced. She'd tried to
wrench Austyn out of her heart because it was the only
way, hoping for a quick if traumatic cure, but she'd only
left herself with a wound which, for all her running away,
wouldn't heal.

Perhaps she'd been wrong. Perhaps the love would
have died naturally if she'd allowed it to bloom. Perhaps.
If. But. Maybe. That was the trouble, she would never
know now, and that was what was bedevilling her so
much. She only knew she wasn't ready to go back. In

her present state of uncertainty it might all start up again, and she'd have wasted a year for nothing.

No, not nothing, Elisa corrected herself. She'd seen a lot of the world, made a lot of friends, filled up lots of sketchbooks which she'd mailed back home. Nothing was ever wasted. Except, a treacherous inner voice contradicted her, a love that was wilfully denied.

Damn the fair-haired man! In some peculiar way he'd set her off on these reflections that were doing her no good at all. She picked up her frayed and battered straw hat and slapped it on her head, as if this decisive movement could bring down a curtain on the past.

OK, so deep down inside she was still bleeding. But it was deep down, hidden, and capable of being forgotten if only she kept herself amused. The rest of her was too healthy, too much alive, to brood and droop for long. 'Laugh and the world laughs with you,' she said aloud. 'Cry and you cry alone.'

'If you say so.' Rich was back beside her, grinning. 'Stop muttering about your lost sleep and look lively. A honeymoon couple who've just seen your ad want to commission you.'

There was something so soothing, so friendly, so uncomplicated about Rich, that Elisa found herself bouncing back to her usual sunny good humour. 'Tell them I'm on my way.'

'Right. Must dash. I've got a few late breakfasters and a smattering of early drinkers.' Rich was off, covering the short distance to the café in a few easy strides.

Elisa took a small mirror from her bag and checked her face. She'd only been on Corfu for a couple of weeks, but her past few months as a seasonal worker in Israel, Crete and Greece had given her an even golden tan that made cosmetics unnecessary. Her indigo eyes and soft pink lips were colour enough.

Apart from brushing particles of the peculiarly gritty sand from her face and re-tying the ribbon on one of her two thick plaits, there was little for her to do. The colour of her hair, pure platinum, was arresting, but it was dead straight, and plaiting it was the easiest way to keep it neat.

All in all, she looked closer to eighteen than twenty-five, not that that was anything to scowl about. It wasn't so long ago when she'd have been considered over the top at her age, on the shelf. Now people thought she chose to stay single. It was funny, the things some people thought...

Smiling to herself, Elisa stood up and slipped on faded denim shorts whose frayed bottoms showed they had once been jeans. Then she buttoned herself into a similarly faded denim shirt with military pockets and epaulettes, rolling up the sleeves in a neat, workmanlike manner.

She left her mat and sandals on the beach and, looking a sexy mixture of competence, self-sufficiency and leggy grace, she was ready to start the day's work. She walked into the café with lengthy, rhythmic strides, not needing to thrust out her bosom or wiggle her hips to catch attention. All the same, there was a certain almost school-girlish exuberance in her walk, coupled with a natural authority that her teaching experience had given her, that would have turned heads even if she'd been as plain as a pikestaff.

Rafe Sinclair's was one of the heads that turned to watch her, his blue eyes chilling without his being aware of it. The old anger stirred, the resentment that had identified her right away for what she was. A spoiler.

The type of girl who drifted into other people's lives with charm and grace and laughter, then drifted out again when she'd got what she wanted, knowing what havoc she'd left behind but not caring.

He felt the pull of her attraction, as everyone did, and despised her for it. He'd wanted such a girl once and she'd wanted him, but he couldn't hold her. No man could. When he'd realised that, he hadn't even tried. Love and disgust didn't go together, not with him, anyway.

Instinctively he looked down at his daughter. She smiled at him uncertainly, as though she sensed his anger and feared she was the cause. He smiled back warmly, reassuringly, but when he looked back at the girl his smile faded.

Elisa went behind the long service counter to get her art materials, and when Rich came past her with a tray of dirty cups and glasses she said, 'Have you heard from Sue? She was still sleeping when I got up this morning, which wasn't surprising because she'd been up most of the night, poor darling.'

'She sent a message saying she's feeling a lot better, but I shouldn't think she'll be up to teaching dancing tonight. It takes a while to get over a bug.'

'I asked why she ate the beefburger in the first place if it was half raw, and she said it was because the sauce was delicious. Crazy novice,' Elisa said, picking up her artboard with beige sugar paper already cut to size and neatly clipped to it, then balancing her box of Conté sticks on top.

'She'll learn. In the meantime——' Rich put down the tray, took one of her plaits and playfully swung it to and fro '—could you cover for her again tonight? She needs the job. She doesn't earn much on the excursion tickets she sells during the day.'

'Sure. I'll be down about ten, all right?'

Rich brushed the end of her plait teasingly over her cheek and nose. 'Elisa, you're as nice as you look. I could so easily fall for you. Just that little bit of encouragement, remember?'

She wrinkled her nose at him, teasing, 'Working with us Brits abroad while you research a thesis on us, huh! That's just a line to learn all our deepest secrets. You're nothing but a beach Casanova.'

'I'd even be a gigolo to please you, love, and why not? You're earning more than the rest of us put together.'

Elisa balanced her art materials on one arm, pulled her plait free and reached up to give his dark hair a playful tug. 'Sorry, Rich, I just can't afford you. I might be doing very nicely at the moment, thank you, but I have to meet my partner in Athens next month and we have a trip to the tiny islands to finance. There won't be any work for us there.'

'Excuses, excuses,' he grumbled. 'Tell you what, I'll do it for nothing.'

'You're supposed to be sacrificing yourself on the altar of sociology, not love,' she pointed out.

'I'm a big fellow. I can spread myself around a bit.'

Elisa smiled. 'Then spread yourself around your customers. Where do I find mine?'

'The far table overlooking the beach. The couple trying very hard to merge two chairs into one.'

Elisa saw them, and as she went back round the counter she saw somebody else. The fair-haired man. He must have been watching the interplay between herself and Rich and disapproving as strongly as when they'd been on the beach, because he was still looking at her as if she'd crawled out from under a stone. Well, it was his hang-up, not hers.

Beside him was the wistful little girl, and next to her was an attractive woman in her thirties, rather formally dressed in a suit of navy blue grosgrain with a yellow blouse. A family group, and not a happy one. What on earth was wrong with them all?

The little girl was sitting closest to the aisle and, as she passed, Elisa impulsively ruffled her fair curls, smiled and said a cheerful 'Hello,' before she walked on. It seemed the friendly thing to do. When she took the spare seat opposite her clients, her back was to the family. Just as well, she thought. The man wouldn't have appreciated her gesture, but her object had been to please his daughter, not him. Five minutes later she was so engrossed in her sketching that she'd forgotten the man and his family. She chatted away, keeping her subjects at their ease to achieve the most natural effect.

Not that this two-shot was hard. They were a good-looking couple, and there was a glow, a unity between them that was easy to capture. She could draw honestly, without the subtle alterations necessary when she sensed her subjects wanted flattery rather than truth.

She unclipped the sketch from the board when she'd finished, saying as she passed it across the table, 'You can buy a frame in Corfu Town or pack it at the bottom of your suitcase with a piece of tissue over it. I hope it's a happy reminder of your honeymoon.'

The patter came so easily now, it was nice to realise she meant it. Nicer still when the bride exclaimed, 'It's great, so much more special than a photograph. Thanks ever so much. We'll really treasure it.'

'Treasure yourselves—stay happy,' Elisa heard herself saying, and thought, Grief, I sound like a maiden aunt!

It was supposed to be a sign of age when policemen looked younger. Nobody had told her brides could have the same effect. Was that why she'd fallen so hard and so unexpectedly for Austyn? Because of good old Anno Domini...some biological clock ticking away deep within her hitting an alarm button to warn she was more than ready.

What an awful thought. It had a soulless touch, and she reacted violently against it. There shouldn't be anything soulless about falling in love. Besides, that didn't explain why Austyn had fallen for her.

She was glad when her clients had finished their exclaiming and the bridegroom began peeling notes from a roll of drachmas. He glanced at her advertisement pinned above the service counter with one of her sketches and, beside it, 'Elisa will draw you for six hundred drachmas'.

'That's twelve hundred drachmas for the two of us, then?' he asked.

'That's right.' Elisa thanked him as she took the money, buttoned it into her shirt pocket, and wished them a happy holiday. As they walked away hand-in-hand she began to pack away her materials, a glance at her watch telling her there was still an hour until noon. She was usually very busy during the lunch-time trade. In the meantime, she'd check on Sue.

She was putting her Conté sticks back into their individual slots in the foam at the bottom of the box when she was conscious of being watched. She looked round and saw the little girl had stolen up silently and was staring at her with painful intensity, her eyes as blue as her father's, but without the ice.

Elisa smiled. 'Hello, have you been there long? I'm sorry I didn't notice you.'

'I've been watching you draw.' Her voice was soft, cultured, hesitant. It was a few seconds before she added, 'You're very clever.'

'It's a knack. I teach art back in England. Do you go to school?'

'I did, but I'm on holiday. A long one.'

'Lucky you.' Elisa smiled, but she wondered about that. It was mid-May, and the long summer holidays weren't due to start for another two months. 'What's your name?'

'Penelope Sinclair. Daddy calls me Penny.'

Sinclair. So that was the man's name. Elisa repeated it to herself, as though trying it for sound. She couldn't think why, nor did she understand why she was glad she'd learned the man's name. He was just another stranger, and a disapproving one at that. His daughter was different again, though. Withdrawn where he was arrogant; uncertain where he was so sure. And, unlike her father, she seemed painfully anxious to be friendly. Elisa looked round at the table where they had been sitting. It was empty of everything but cups and Penny's scarcely touched milkshake. 'All by yourself?' she asked cheerfully.

'Yes. Daddy said I could stay so long as I didn't go away.'

Elisa kept to herself the thought that the sad little mite seemed to be *in* the way. She seemed so lonely. 'Don't you get bored all by yourself?'

'I'd be bored in the hotel,' Penny explained, quaintly serious. She pointed along the beach to where pedal-boats were drawn up on the sand. The honeymoon couple had just hired one and their laughter floated back as they launched it and jumped in. 'Here I can watch the boats. They look such fun.'

'They are. You must ask Daddy to take you out in one.'

'Oh, no. I mustn't be a nuisance.' The words weren't spoken resentfully, but as though they were a fact of life.

The louse, Elisa thought. Not only to me and the world in general, but to his little girl. The flash of anger must have shown in her eyes, because Penny asked nervously, 'Am I being a nuisance to you?'

Elisa swallowed her rage and smiled. 'Certainly not.' She wavered, thinking she really should visit Sue before she became busy again, but had no defence against those wistful eyes. 'Would you like to sit down and keep me company? I've got nothing to do just now.'

'Thank you,' Penny said primly, and quietly sat on the chair opposite hers.

She's not natural, Elisa thought. She's like a little old lady. Where was the sparkle, the noise, the restlessness of childhood? She couldn't be a day over six, and she was behaving with more circumspection than a sixty-year-old.

Elisa heard a clatter of crockery and looked round to see Rich clearing away the cups from the empty table. 'Rich,' she called, 'will you bring that milkshake over here?'

'Sure.' He brought it over, smiling. 'Got a new customer?'

'No,' Elisa corrected. 'This is Penny. She's more important than a customer. She's a friend.'

She was rewarded when Penny smiled. It was a very shy smile, but it was a beginning. The smile widened when Rich said, 'Hello, Penny. Can I be a friend, too?'

He held out his hand and Elisa's heart warmed to him as Penny put her hand into his and they solemnly shook. Either he'd noticed the child was lonely or he just couldn't help being nice. She smiled herself as he said, 'Richard Kenwood at your service, but now we're friends you can call me Rich.'

'Not *Uncle* Rich?' Penny asked dubiously.

'Gosh, no, that's much too stuffy. Well, ladies, I'll have to leave you to your gossip. I have work to do.'

Another big smile and he was gone. 'He's nice,' Penny said, then just sat there looking at Elisa as though that were occupation enough.

When really, Elisa thought, she should be on the beach making friends, sandcastles, noise! Yet there was something expectant, hopeful, about her. 'Would you like me to draw you?' she guessed.

'Yes, please.'

The answer was so prompt Elisa had to smile. Any other child would have come right out with it, not waited for an offer that might never have been made. She settled back in her chair with her artboard on her lap and said, 'Sit how you feel most comfortable. Right, here we go.'

She sketched quickly, knowing how fidgety children could be. Penny, though, was the exception. She was too still, too stiff, so Elisa began her usual relaxing questions. 'Are you staying at the hotel?'

'No. Daddy's house is in the mountains.'

'Ah. So he's brought you to the beach for the day?'

'No,' Penny corrected again. 'He was taking me and Miss Tilson to town. We stopped here for tea because Miss Tilson wasn't feeling well. The tea didn't work, so Daddy's taken her into the hotel to lie down. When she's better, he's taking us home so she can rest properly.'

It sounded to Elisa as though somebody else had been eating underdone beefburgers. She guessed, 'Is Miss Tilson your nanny?'

'Yes.'

'I expect you call her Tilly, don't you?'

'Oh, no. She wouldn't like that. It wouldn't be polite.'

It would be a darned sight more friendly, Elisa thought, but she held her peace. Afraid her questions were drifting away from relaxing chatter and into outright prying, she changed the subject. 'Did you know Penelope is a Greek name?'

'Yes. Mummy and Daddy met here a long time ago. That's why they chose it.'

And why they came back to Corfu, Elisa supposed. A special island with special connections. Perhaps each return was a renewal of their love. Perhaps, and she felt a twinge of compassion, they loved each other to the exclusion of all else, including their child. Penny didn't look as though much love and laughter had strayed her way.

Come to think of it, neither did her father. Something was wrong somewhere. She'd put two and two together and hadn't come up with half an answer. She *had* finished the sketch, though. It seemed to have drawn itself while her mind had wandered where it had no business to be.

She saw with dismay that it was much, much too honest. The soft little mouth drooped wistfully, the large eyes were full of apprehensive appeal. My God, Elisa thought, if she were a puppy she wouldn't even have to raise a begging paw to break my heart.

She was wondering whether to tear it up and draw something less painfully observant when the outlines blurred and another face seemed to grow out of it, stronger and full of challenging anger.

Sinclair, the child's father.

Well, let him be angry. If it took an artist's eyes to show him what he should see for himself, perhaps the jolt would do him good, teach him something. She saw again those cold, dismissive eyes. He hadn't bothered to hide his unmerited scorn of her. Why should she bother to hide her merited scorn of him as a father?

It was tit for tat, and he would be the loser. She felt a tiny tingle at the bottom of her spine that crept icily up to her scalp, making her give an involuntary shiver. It was suspiciously like fear... a warning he didn't look like a man who lost easily.

To hell with him. Decisively she unclipped the sketch and passed it over to Penny. The child didn't see any messages in it, she just exclaimed, 'It's—it's *me*.'

Elisa smiled, her strange apprehension gone as though it had never been. 'That's the nicest compliment you could pay me.'

It was an unfortunate choice of words. At the mention of 'pay' Penny became the formal little lady again. 'I must see Daddy. It says in the advertisement a sketch costs six hundred drachmas.'

'So you can read...' Elisa began.

'Of course I can. I'm six and I've been reading for ages.'

'Ah, well, if you're six and can read, you should also be able to listen,' Elisa continued teasingly, then wondered what on earth she'd said. Penny's brief animation fled. She sat up straight, almost bristling with attention, that puppy-dog anxiety filling her eyes again.

Elisa sighed, baffled, and explained, 'I only wanted to say you don't owe me anything. I only charge customers. You're a *friend*.'

'Oh!' The smile, the sparkle, was back, but by now Elisa was resigned to its vanishing. She was right. Penny climbed down from her chair, saying, 'It was very nice to meet you, Elisa. I mustn't stay any longer or I *will* be a nuisance, won't I?'

'You could never be a nuisance. Perhaps you'd better let your father know you haven't wandered away, though.'

'Yes, and I want to show him my picture.' A grave smile, and she walked primly away.

Elisa shook her head, mystified, then went behind the counter at the same time as Rich to put her art materials away. He poured two ouzos and lemonade for customers and a third for her. 'On the house,' he murmured, 'while the boss is away. I reckon he's got a nerve to charge you commission. You attract customers to the place.'

'It's fair enough. I take up chair space while I'm working, after all.' Elisa put three hundred drachmas in the commission box and picked up the long, cool drink he'd poured for her. 'Thanks, I could do with something with a kick in it. Bring me back to the twentieth century.'

Rich's mobile eyebrows shot up questioningly. 'Come again?'

'You're never going to believe this, but that little girl is pure Victorian. As our resident sociology expert, what do you make of that?'

'Must get it from her father. He didn't approve of us having a bit of fun in the sun, did he?'

'I wonder why?' Elisa mused.

'Probably jealous. I would have been if you'd been rolling around in the sand with him.'

'Not much chance of that.' She meant to laugh, but somehow she couldn't quite manage it. She felt too strangely—wistful. How ridiculous! Pulling herself together, she added, 'Besides, neither of you have the least right to be jealous of who I roll in the sand with— not that I make a practice of it.'

Rich picked up his tray with the drinks on and manoeuvred carefully past her. 'Men are men, darling, and rights don't come into it when the old green-eyed monster rears its ugly head.'

'His eyes are blue.'

'Whose?'

'Sinclair's. Penny's father.'

Rich paused and looked at her searchingly. The banter dropped from his voice as he said, 'I hope you haven't forgotten there's a wife in the picture somewhere. I know the woman with him was only the nanny, but...'

'Of course I haven't forgotten,' Elisa broke in, forcing a laugh that should have come easily. 'I'm not interested in the man.'

'Oh?'

Elisa flushed slightly at the doubt in his voice. 'No, not interested, more sort of intrigued.'

'That's worse.'

'All I meant was I can't understand why he seemed to disapprove of me so much.'

'You? I thought it was us?'

'Whatever.' Elisa was annoyed she'd got herself into this and sought for a way out. 'Rich, you're beginning to sound as Victorian as that little girl.'

'You mean this isn't the time to point out that the sun, foreign soil, escape from responsibility, tanned bodies, spiked drinks at midday and all that jazz can do funny things to people?'

'I mean it isn't necessary. I'm not the novice abroad, and my drink had better not be spiked. Ouzo doesn't need it, thanks very much,' she retorted.

'I think you're ducking the issue, darling.'

'Oh, go and twirl your side-whiskers! I'm going to finish my drink on the beach, then check on Sue—and God help any other nit-picking men who cross my path today.' Elisa wanted to stride off, but she strolled, just to let Rich know he was stirring up a storm in a teacup.

It was really hot now, and oiled bodies were stretched out all over the place. Elisa's own particular space, secured by her beach mat and sandals, had been respected. She sat down, fanning her over-heated face with her frayed hat.

After a while, honesty compelled her to admit *she* was the one being ridiculous and that Rich was right, Sinclair was a no-go area. That was no problem. Sinclair might have given her a funny look, but that was all it was, and since when had she been over-sensitive?

Probably he always looked like that when he found himself unexpectedly slumming in a package-holiday resort, the snob! What a lot of fun he must miss, to say nothing of his little girl.

Elisa, sipping her drink and sighing, wanted to forget all about the Sinclairs. The problem was, they wouldn't go away. She found herself puzzling over Penny and frowning over her father. The one was quaint while the other was——

She was still trying to figure out the right word for Sinclair when she was conscious of somebody standing over her. She raised her hat to shield her eyes from the sun and, expecting it to be Rich, she smiled to show she had returned to her normal sunny self.

It was Sinclair.

She was instantly alert, but somehow she wasn't surprised. It worried her, not being surprised. Had she known in her bones they would tangle again? Last time they'd duelled with their eyes...or, at least, he had. This time she hoped for something pleasanter, something more civilised and normal, so she could push him out of her mind.

One look in his eyes and her hopes died a sudden death. They were as icy as ever. So he hadn't liked the sketch. Well, she hadn't expected him to, had she?

'Your fee,' he said.

Elisa rose to her feet in one fluid movement. She didn't want to argue from an inferior position, not that there should be an argument. She still found herself looking up to him but there wasn't anything she could do about that. 'No, that's not necessary. I offered to draw Penny, I wasn't asked. I did explain to her about that.'

She might have saved her breath. 'Six hundred drachmas,' he went on, 'that's less than three pounds sterling. Anybody who works as cheaply as you do really can't afford to work for nothing.'

Elisa gasped. The implication was that *she* was cheap. The nerve of the man. All her pacific impulses shrivelled and she said angrily, 'Spend the money on a pedal-boat ride for Penny. She's the one in need, not me. Who knows, you might actually bring a smile to her face, poor little thing! As her father, you should find that more rewarding than trying to take the smile off mine.'

She saw the anger glow in his eyes and thought, Good heavens, nobody ever told me ice could burn. But he wasn't the sort of man to lose control, and he sounded more impatient than anything when he said, 'You appear to have trouble running your own business, so I don't think it's advisable to interfere with mine.'

Then he took her hat out of her hand, put it on her head, curled her fingers around the drachmas and held them there. 'As I was saying, your fee.'

At his touch a surge of feeling shot up her arm and radiated over her entire body. There was nothing fierce about the way his hand closed over hers, and yet she felt as though she were being assaulted and embraced at the same time. It was exciting, frightening—and humiliating to know he could have this effect on her.

She could only hope there was a short circuit somewhere and he couldn't sense what he was doing to her. She said, more breathlessly than she cared for, 'When you've quite finished with my hand, I'd like to have it back. We've been attached to each other for a long time.'

He released her and now she couldn't read his expression at all, not that he gave her much chance. His mission accomplished, he turned and walked away. Elisa stared after him, then sat down rather suddenly.

A brunette close by, one of a group of girls sunbathing topless, raised her head and said with an irrepressible Geordie accent, 'Half your luck, love. I wouldn't mind a bit of that myself.'

Elisa smiled weakly. She felt weak all over. Perversely, she was angrier with herself than with Sinclair. First she'd been over-sensitive, now she was over-reacting. What was the matter with her. *There was a wife somewhere!* Besides, she didn't like him and he didn't like her.

Burning ice, indeed! How puerile. Whoever heard of ice that burned? And yet...and yet she felt scorched and she had the shocking feeling Sinclair knew it. 'Little girls who play with fire...' she breathed, mocking herself, trying to kid herself out of it. That didn't do much good so she changed it to, 'Little girls on the rebound...'

That did the trick but, for a moment, her face was as wistful as little Penny's had been.

Walking through the café, the garden and into the hotel, Rafe Sinclair was thinking: deep-water eyes. She had deep-water eyes. Not the turquoise or aquamarine of the shallows, but the mysterious indigo that could only be found far out in the bay.

And he didn't like the way they haunted him, those deep-water eyes.

CHAPTER TWO

ELISA was moody that afternoon, full of contradictions. She didn't want to be on her own, but she didn't feel particularly sociable, either. She knew why, and that only made her moodier.

Her brush with Sinclair, infuriating as it had been, had stimulated and unsettled her. She wasn't masochistic enough to want to meet him again, but somehow everything had become flat and boring, including people she'd previously found interesting.

Austyn had made her feel the same way.

Drat Austyn. Drat Sinclair. Drat Richard's thesis, which he was expounding again for her and Sue's benefit. Sue, still too tottery after her bout of food poisoning to work, but no longer ill enough to lie in bed, was all attention. Rich was a very attractive man.

Elisa was finding it difficult to concentrate or contribute anything to Rich's ideas. The three of them were drinking coffee in a café farther along the beach, squandering the couple of hours he had off duty. It seemed a bit of a busman's holiday to Elisa, but the other two were perfectly content.

They had planned to take out a pedal-boat, with Rich and herself doing the work and Sue relaxing on the back, but the weather had turned again. The winter and spring rains which made this jewel of an island so green and fertile should have ended last month, but this was proving to be a very wet May.

28

The sky was overcast again, a downpour was imminent and Elisa was trying hard not to drum her fingers on the table. She was a doer, not a dreamer, and inaction bugged her at the best of times. She wished it wouldn't seem so rude if she just got up and walked away.

She turned her head towards the sea at the sudden sound of a speed-boat gunning across the water. A man was standing on the platform anchored out in the bay, attached by a harness both to the boat and the multi-coloured parachute stretched out behind him. The boat zoomed away, the parachute filled and the man soared into the air.

Parascending. A sport she loved and could easily become addicted to. She wished she were up there now. Unfortunately, it was an expensive form of escapism for somebody saving to finance further travel.

Elisa smothered a sigh and tried to pay attention to the discussion. Sue was a bouncy little brunette and her brown eyes were glowing into Rich's as she told him, 'I think you're frightfully clever, but I honestly can't see what's interesting enough about us seasonal workers to put into a thesis.'

'You're a fascinating bunch,' he assured her. 'On the surface you're such different types and you give apparently differing reasons for working abroad, but when I've enough case histories on record I suspect an overall pattern and motivation will emerge.'

'Oh,' Sue said doubtfully, 'I think you've lost me somewhere.'

'OK, what does a medical secretary from a comfortable home have in common with a dole drop-out from an underprivileged background, or a computer programmer with a bricklayer?'

'Not a lot,' Sue replied after some consideration.

'The first thing they have in common is that back home they wouldn't dream of doing menial work for long hours, precious little pay and living accommodation that's inadequate to say the least. They'd regard the work as beneath them and scream of exploitation, among other things, if they were forced to do it. Yet they come out here to do it willingly and call it fun. Why?'

Sue, the medical secretary he'd referred to, shrugged. 'Everything's different abroad, isn't it? Must be the sun.'

Rich smiled. 'It's more than that. You're all running— either away from something you don't like, or to something you haven't found yet. In some cases, both.' His eyes flicked to Elisa as he concluded, 'Some people know they're running, others don't. In any case, it's a social pattern that's providing me with some fascinating research.'

Elisa had caught his look and the speculation in it. Rich suspected she'd kept back more than she'd revealed when he'd interviewed her, and he was too dedicated a researcher to be satisfied with less than the truth.

She didn't want to go under the microscope again. She was still in a funny mood, feeling things she didn't want to be honest about even to herself. To sidetrack him, she said, 'Aren't you forgetting the rootless young isn't a modern phenomenon? Maybe we're subconsciously obeying a primitive urge to migrate. I mean, the world wasn't always settled, was it? Maybe we've become so civilised, we simply don't recognise the urge to move on for what it really is.'

'How come everybody doesn't take off when spring comes and the weather's suitable?' Rich asked.

'Some of us are more primitive than others,' Elisa hazarded. She was talking off the top of her head and didn't want to defend an idea she'd thrown out as a hopeful red herring, and nothing more.

'An interesting theory,' Rich acknowledged. 'What are your thoughts on it, Sue?'

Sue didn't have any thoughts beyond how dishy Rich was, but she wasn't going to disappoint him so she began talking anyway. Far from relaxing, Elisa was increasingly hard put to it not to fidget. She wanted to get away, not from Rich and Sue particularly, but from herself.

She recognised the symptoms well enough to diagnose the sickness. It was Sinclair. The man was married, disagreeable and disinterested. A complete turn-off from any point of view. She could live with him raising her hackles. That was normal, given the sort of person he was. What she couldn't live with was him getting under her skin. That was abnormal, given the sort of person she was. And leaping out of the frying pan into the fire just wasn't in it!

Sue paused for breath. Elisa silently blessed her, seized her chance and stood up. 'I think I'll make a dash for the shops before the rain starts,' she said. 'While I'm up there, I think I'll get some work in, too.'

Sue, predictably, didn't protest, but Rich said, 'You're keen. You had enough customers at lunch time to last a week.'

'Nothing like striking while the iron's on the sizzle,' she replied, giving him a big grin she hoped didn't have 'deceit' printed all over it.

But Rich, besides being handsome and nice, was also sensitive. 'Is everything all right? I've never known you so quiet.'

'You mean that with a chatterbox like me it shows.' She laughed but he didn't join in, just continued to watch her with thoughtful eyes. Blast you, Rich, she thought.

Why do you have to be perceptive? If I'd fallen for you, I'd be charmed, but since I haven't you're just irritating me. Let me go without a fuss, there's a honey.

It wasn't Rich's day to be a honey, because he continued, 'Quiet and restless. An intriguing combination.' He stressed the 'intriguing' slightly so that she was reminded of how she'd told him, when she'd denied any interest in Sinclair, that she'd merely been intrigued.

She had to let it pass. If Rich knew she'd made the connection he really would be suspicious. Just because she'd felt like a maiden aunt once that day was no reason for encouraging him to turn into a kindly uncle. She didn't need a lecture. She could deliver a pretty telling one herself.

'Quiet, restless and intriguing,' she mused, making a joke of it. 'Great. Maybe it will improve my artistic charisma. Anything rather than cut an ear off like Van Gogh.'

Another smile and she moved off, taking a narrow path that meandered around newly built hotels sited at all sorts of angles to the beach, past agricultural plots and small fenced-off lemon groves, until it emerged eventually at the tarmacked coastal road.

As Rich had once observed, half the little resort looked as though it were falling down and the other half looked as though it were being built up. It was the charmingly muddled effect of an ancient agricultural-fishing community transforming itself into a far more lucrative tourist industry.

Nobody had given a thought to pavements, and walking along the narrow road where the cafés in front of the hotels edged it on either side was rather like dicing with death. The Corfiots, from what Elisa had observed, drove like maniacs, and she stopped several times to press herself against the wall of a café or bar as cars, coaches and huge delivery lorries hurtled past with apparently scant regard for pedestrians or each other.

Elisa cheered up as she answered a constant stream of greetings from holidaymakers she'd sketched, seasonal workers who included her in their close-knit community, and Corfiots who welcomed her as an asset into their cafés and encouraged her efforts to speak Greek.

She'd made herself a profitable niche in this friendly, carefree little resort. She had advertisements up in several cafés, but it was word-of-mouth recommendations that brought her more work than she'd dreamed of.

She was doing so well, she'd decided to use the resort as a base from which to explore the island instead of moving on every few days to start up all over again, as she'd originally intended.

Now she wasn't so sure. Much as she wanted to stay and exploit her success, all her instincts told her to run. The frying pan and the fire analogy had sent warning shivers up her spine. Already emotionally weak from frustrated longings, she had a horror of becoming involved on the rebound.

So many women did that, then awoke one morning to find a man beside them they'd only imagined they'd loved, because the emotion suppressed inside them had to spill over somewhere.

Elisa didn't want that to happen to her, especially with a man like Sinclair. He might be taboo, but her uneasiness was caused by the conviction that they hadn't finished with each other yet.

No, she didn't want Sinclair, love on the rebound or anything like that. She just wanted time to heal properly. When she was whole, she wouldn't have to take fright when she felt this alertness, this tingling tension in all her senses. She would be able to trust love, and herself—but it had to be with an eligible and uncomplicated man.

Fate, she felt, owed her that much.

What fate sent her right then was a torrential downpour that had her racing into the nearest café. The awning outside, and her speed, kept her and her art materials dry, and it wasn't long before she was busy sketching. The rain didn't last long and then the sun shone again with steaming brilliance.

The brolly-and-bikini weather continued throughout the rest of the afternoon and evening. Elisa sketched on, using work as a therapy, trying to close by mental effort the vulnerable chink Sinclair had pierced in her emotional defences.

When she felt hungry she walked away from the bustling tourist development and climbed the incredibly steep track to the tranquillity of the old village. She passed between pastel and whitewashed houses clinging to the hillside and each other like so many tiered cubes that hadn't been properly stacked.

She came to her favourite little restaurant, where she dined cheaply and well on moussaka, fruit and a local wine that wasn't half as rough as some of the stuff sold in fancy bottles at her supermarket back home.

She should have been content. In fact she was as restless as ever.

Irritated with herself as much as anything, Elisa walked down the hill to her tiny whitewashed room that reminded her of nothing so much as a monk's cell. When she'd changed into a loose black sweater and a colourful Indian cotton skirt, she joined Rich to teach Greek dancing to the hardy souls who braved the chill damp air to finish their night's entertainment at the beach café.

It was past two in the morning when Elisa fell into bed, exhausted and exasperated. She'd spent the entire evening searching for one particular face and feeling both gladness and sorrow when she didn't see it. She woke late to a cloudless sky, a fierce sun that had the promise of permanence about it, a headache and a resolution to stop being such a silly fool.

She took the day off, hired a scooter and headed for the hills. By the time she came back down again, she reckoned, she'd have exorcised her ghosts.

She rode sedately, mindful of the grisly lecture Rich had delivered along with the full English breakfast she'd ordered at the café.

'Only the mentally deficient ride scooters on these roads,' he told her. 'Do you know how many accidents there have been on them, how many lives lost? Inexperienced idiots hire them and go joyriding over tracks meant only for goats. I tell you, those scooters are notorious out here.'

'I'm not inexperienced. I used a scooter to get to school when I was doing my A-levels.'

'That was a long time ago,' Rich pointed out.

'Thanks very much. You're a great ego booster at breakfast. Well, in my decrepit state I won't be doing any joyriding, will I? No, just pottering along as befits my age, and stopping now and again to do some sketching.'

But there was no kidding Rich out of his doom and gloom. He grumbled, 'I know you. You'll be so entranced by the shape of a tree, you won't see a hole in the road until you fall into it. Look at you, bare legs and flimsy blouse, no protection for your skin if you do come off. And who's going to help you? Wait until I can wangle a day off and I'll come with you.'

'Rich!' she'd protested, laughing. 'If I listen to you much longer I'll shoot back to bed for fear I trip and break my neck. You're making me a nervous wreck. If I were the fragile little goose you seem to think me, I'd have fled back to England months ago.'

He hadn't been amused, but Elisa smiled reflectively as she headed south, then turned off along a dirt road that looked as though it might lead somewhere interesting. She'd no set destination in mind, meaning to wander wherever her fancy took her.

She felt comfortable in her well-worn cut-offs and open-necked blouse, and scarcely felt the weight of the little haversack slung over her back containing her lunch, a sweater, sketchbook and sketching sticks. It was a windless day, but she was travelling just fast enough to stir up a breeze. It lifted the heavy hair from her neck, creating a nice feeling of freedom after having worn it in plaits for so long. There was no need for her to be neat today.

The track climbed steadily, wide enough for two cars to pass at a pinch, until she was well into the hills. She hadn't passed a thing, although she'd seen an occasional worker in the olive groves, and passed an occasional house. Rich had been right about the roads, and she had to swerve to avoid ruts now and again, but the peace and solitude soothed her spirit while the freedom of action and movement the scooter gave her satisfied her restlessness.

Maybe it's not Sinclair at all, she thought. Maybe I've really turned into a nomad, and a fortnight in one place has become too long. Maybe...

Her thoughts came to an abrupt end as she saw a small figure appear at the bend ahead and trudge towards her. Elisa was surprised. She hadn't passed any type of habitation for some time, and certainly no small child without an adult close by. She slowed down then stopped as she recognised the little face and unmistakable fair curly hair of Penny Sinclair.

'Penny!' she exclaimed. 'Where do you think you're going?'

'Hello!' Penny's face lit up and she ran over to her. 'I'm looking for the sea. I want to watch the pedal-boats.'

'You can't walk to the sea. It's much too far.'

'I know, but there's a gap in the trees somewhere where the sea shows through. I've seen it from Daddy's car, only I've been walking for ages and I can't find it.'

Elisa had passed a place about two miles back where it was possible to look down over the hills to the sea far beyond, although the beach and the pedal-boats certainly weren't visible.

'It's too far for you to walk, Penny. Where's your father?'

'At his office in Corfu Town. He left very early this morning.'

'And Miss Tilson?' Elisa asked.

'She's lying down. She said I should lie down, too, but I'm not sleepy, so I came out to look for the sea.'

'Then nobody knows where you are? Oh, Penny, she might be looking all over for you.'

The child shook her head. 'She took some pills. She sleeps for ages when she takes those.'

'Is she still ill?'

'I don't think so. She told Daddy she was better.'

Elisa looked at her watch. She'd been late setting out on her trip because she'd got up late, but it still wasn't quite midday. A bit early for a siesta. 'Is there anybody else at home to look after you?' she asked.

'There's Mrs Pappas. That's what we call her because her real name is very long and complicated. She's our housekeeper but she lives at the farm, not with us. She comes in the mornings and lets me help in the kitchen. That's fun, only she's gone home now and won't be back until this evening.'

'I'd better take you home, then,' Elisa told her. 'Your daddy won't want you wandering around on your own like this.' He probably won't like me taking you home either, she thought caustically, but there's not a lot I can do about that.

'Oh, Elisa, please can I look at the sea first? Please, just one tiny peep.'

Elisa looked at the hopeful little face and discovered she was softer than she'd thought. 'All right, then, one quick look and straight home again—and you must promise you won't wander off if your nanny is still asleep.'

Penny's face flushed with pleasure. 'I promise. Thank you. Goodbye.' And she started trudging on again.

'Not by yourself!' Elisa called, turning the scooter and moving her haversack round to her front. 'Hop on, hang on and sit still. Got that?'

Penny did as she was told, saying excitedly, 'I've never been on a scooter before and my feet *are* tired. I didn't think it would be so far. It's so quick in Daddy's car.'

Elisa started off slowly and rode steadily back the way she had come, with Penny squealing with pleasure behind her. It was the first time she'd behaved like a normal little girl. When they came to the gap in the trees Elisa cut the motor, put her feet down on either side of the scooter and said, 'There's your sea, Penny. If you put your hands on my shoulders and stand on the pillion, you'll see much better.'

Penny stood up. 'I can't see the beach or the pedal-boats.'

'No, I'm afraid those lower hills are in the way. Disappointed?'

'N-no. The sea's lovely and blue, and the scooter's fun.'

'Right, down you get and I'll take you home.' Elisa heard a car and looked away from the sea to the road ahead.

Penny hadn't had time to get down, and she gave a little hop of surprise. 'It's my daddy.'

The scooter wobbled. Elisa steadied it as a dusty Land Rover drew level and stopped. Sinclair jumped out. He was wearing the trousers of his lightweight business suit, but he'd taken off his jacket and tie. The top buttons of his blue and white striped shirt were undone and the sleeves rolled up above his elbows.

He looked very male. He ignored her, giving all his attention to his daughter. 'Hello, Penny,' he said, plucking her from the pillion and swinging her into the Land Rover, 'you're a long way from home.'

'I wanted to see the sea and Elisa gave me a ride. It was such *fun*.'

'Was it, indeed?' he murmured non-committally, then he shut the door and came back to Elisa. 'Who gave you permission to put my daughter on that damned deathtrap?' he asked.

His voice was so quiet, she didn't realise immediately he was keeping his anger under control for Penny's sake, and she answered innocently, 'Nobody, actually, but——'

'I thought not,' he broke in, and then she became aware of the menace beneath his careful control. 'I don't know what you're doing up here and I don't much care, but if I ever see my daughter on that bike again, I'll wrap it around a tree before you get a chance to. Do I make myself clear?'

He didn't wait for an answer. He jumped into the Land Rover and drove on before she could get out a single word of explanation. The irony was that Penny turned round to smile and wave.

For long seconds Elisa stayed where she was, stunned and furious. Then she started the engine and took off, not in her original direction, because that would mean turning to follow his car, but back the way she'd come.

If there was one thing worse than having one's best intentions misinterpreted, it was being given no chance to defend oneself. The man was a bad-tempered, autocratic, petty dictator. She hadn't wanted to meet him again, anyway, and now she'd ride all around the island if necessary to avoid him.

Suddenly the white heat of her rage turned into a cold sweat. He didn't—he couldn't possibly!—think she'd come up here in the hope of meeting him again. Certainly Penny had told her they lived in the hills, but there were hundreds of them. It was only the whim of the moment that had brought her this way.

Was his ego such he thought she'd wangled specific directions out of Penny when she'd sketched her at the café? It didn't seem credible, but then neither did her clashes with the man himself.

Humiliation flooded her cheeks with fresh colour, and when she found a narrow track leading off to the right she turned into it. Anything to get away from the road and any further possible contact with Sinclair.

Elisa found herself doing the sort of rough riding Rich had deplored, round boulders, through pebbly streams, bouncing over lumps and bumps, skidding on sudden turns, and needing all her concentration to keep herself and the machine together.

Occasionally she passed a humble farm dwelling, wandering goats with incredibly long silky white coats and once, amazingly, a Corfiot coming the other way on a scooter with a black and white collie sitting nonchalantly between his legs. The man raised a hand in a casual salute, which was more than Elisa dared do, although she managed a smile.

Eventually, and much to her surprise, she emerged between sand dunes on to a beach of fine white sand that stretched as far as she could see without a solitary soul or building in sight. She hadn't a clue where she was and she didn't much care.

Her legs shaking after the tension of her wild ride, her emotions in a turmoil, she left the scooter and walked along the beach muttering things that would have put the curl back into Sinclair's cropped hair if he could have heard them. After a while she calmed down enough to sit down, and that was where she stayed for the rest of the afternoon.

Which was why, when Sinclair drove back along the road looking for her, he couldn't find her.

CHAPTER THREE

BACK in her room that evening, shampooed and showered and dressing to go out, Elisa was reflecting grimly on a wasted day. No ghosts had been exorcised, quite the reverse. The empty beach had offered precious little worth sketching, and she had doodled wistful images of Austyn.

That was normal enough when she wasn't fully occupied, but it had come as a jolt to find Sinclair staring up at her from the page. His cold eyes seemed to be challenging her with questions she had no answers for, and so she'd closed the pad and sketched no more.

The accuracy of the sketch still haunted her. No more than three brief encounters with the man, each of them charged with enough emotion to warp her judgement, yet she'd drawn his face as surely as if she'd known it for years. And she hadn't even known she was doing it.

It was frightening, all the more so because she couldn't shrug it off. Little as she wanted to, she had to think it through and she didn't like the conclusion she came to. It was as though, subconsciously, she and Sinclair had recognised each other as enemies from the start. That accounted for the antagonism that crackled between them like static electricity.

But it didn't account for the attraction that flared as fiercely as the antagonism, two opposing forces that only flowed together in a male-female confrontation. A confrontation she didn't want and neither, she was sure, did Sinclair. So where did that leave them?

Out on a limb, Elisa reflected sourly, her least favourite position.

She wasn't strong enough yet to face up to this kind of situation. Emotionally, she still classified herself as walking wounded. One more clout and she could very well go down for the count. Unless, of course, she clouted back, but she couldn't see Sinclair crumbling. He had his arrogance to protect him. And his ego. And his contempt.

How dared he be contemptuous of her? Everything seemed to come back to that. Within her some reckless streak was raring to meet the challenge, gaining strength with each new provocation so that she was losing more and more control. She was within an ace of throwing out a challenge of her own, and to blazes with the consequences. The passive role had never suited her.

Belatedly it occurred to her that Sinclair might have succeeded where she had failed, and dismissed their clashes from his mind. Somehow she didn't think so, and she would soon know if she was right. He would come looking for her. He wouldn't be able to help himself. What happened then would be entirely up to her.

No wonder she was a bag of nerves.

She was also, much to her surprise, ready to go out. Lost in thought, she had none the less dressed in her usual evening garb of faded, tapered jeans and loose black sweater. Travelling with a backpack limited her choice of clothes, just as it put a stop to impulse shopping. There was no point in accumulating things she couldn't carry.

The tiny room, behind a taverna, which she rented for three pounds a night was dark, with the solitary window shuttered for privacy, and the light from the bare electric bulb suspended from the ceiling gleamed on her newly washed hair. She had parted it in the centre and it fell in thick, soft tresses about her face and shoulders.

She added a touch of duty-free perfume to her throat, slung a denim jacket over her shoulder and looked at her watch. Seven-thirty. An hour until sunset. She meant to finish her day off by not working tonight, and decided to walk along the beach until she felt hungry.

She didn't particularly want to be alone, but it seemed best. Her thoughts were not the sort she could share with anybody. She switched off the light and opened the door. The last of the day's sunshine should have flooded into the room, but there was a large shape there, obstructing it.

Sinclair.

Elisa jumped and stepped back. Then she stood quite still, surveying him with an almost fatalistic calm. There was no sense in being twee or fluttery or deceitful any more. She'd known all along that they couldn't back off from each other, much as they might want to. And, since it was a moment of truth, she was ready to admit to herself that her apparently harmless trip into the hills had been a subconscious search for him.

This revelation annoyed her so much that she felt a new surge of antagonism towards him. She didn't like to feel helpless. That wasn't the way she ran her life at all. Nor did she like the calm way he was surveying her, looking casually classy in dark brown trousers and loose-ribbed cream sweater, and in no hurry to explain how he had found her and why he should want to.

His eyes were strictly neutral. No ice, no warmth, nothing but this almost clinical appraisal. What was he looking for, the jugular? And did he think she was going to stand here all night while he gave her the twice-over?

He looked past her into the tiny room with its narrow bed, rickety chest of drawers and few inches of bare floor space between the two. Elisa's irritation increased and she said coldly, 'When you've quite finished...'

'I didn't come to fight,' he replied evenly. 'I came to apologise.'

That was the last thing she was expecting, and she cursed him silently. He'd taken her by surprise again. She said, as crisply as she could, 'For what? Looking at me as though I'm some form of low life, intimating I blackmail parents into paying for uncommissioned sketches, or assuming I wilfully endanger children's lives?'

'You sound as if you have a persecution complex.'

'I have,' Elisa agreed with false pleasantness. 'It developed the minute I met you. I'd call it justified, but naturally that's just my opinion.'

She saw his eyebrows draw together and was grimly satisfied. She didn't need to be told he wasn't the type who apologised easily, if ever, and presumably she was supposed to be grateful for his condescension. Well, she wasn't, and now he knew it.

'Actually we haven't met, not officially,' Sinclair pointed out.

'Fancy me missing a blessing like that,' she marvelled, and moved to walk past him. 'Now, if you'll excuse me...'

His arm shot across the doorway, barring her exit, and she walked straight into it. She felt the roughness of his sweater against her throat, but she was too angry to move back. She just turned her head and glared up at him. It was a mistake, because he was looking down and their faces were very close. She felt a betraying flutter of her senses as he said quietly, 'I really am sorry. On all three counts.'

Elisa moved back then, knowing she'd lose any advantage she'd gained if she stayed so close to him. It was easier to loathe Sinclair from a distance. The slightest touch between them and the issue became confused. She said huffily, 'That's all very well, but why pick on me in the first place? Whatever have I done to you?'

'Shall we discuss it over dinner? I really would like to make amends. I'm very grateful for you stopping Penny from straying too far today. When I knew what really happened I came back looking for you, but you'd vanished. That's why I'm here tonight.'

Elisa thought of her wild ride when she'd left the road, trying to recapture all the antagonism she'd felt towards him then. It was slipping away fast, and she needed it to protect herself from him. Somehow she sensed he'd sought her out merely for form's sake. She'd helped his child and she had to be thanked because it was the proper thing to do, but beneath his present courtesy his antagonism towards her was undiminished.

She couldn't voice these doubts without sounding paranoid, so she said, 'I only did what anyone would have done. There's no need for any "amends".'

'I think I'm the best judge of that.'

Elisa was no raving feminist, but his cool assumption flicked her to the raw. 'When you're not being thoroughly nasty,' she told him furiously, 'you're a pompous ass.'

She struck his arm away and went to go past him. He caught her by the shoulders and swung her round so that she was facing him, and when she tried to pull away she found her back was pressed against the door-jamb. His hands were hurting her, but she knew she couldn't free herself without a degrading struggle she was bound to lose.

She just had to stand there while he got himself under control, and that startled her, because he gave the impression of a man who never lost control. But he was bending towards her, their faces only an inch or so apart, and as she read his expression she knew she'd cut through the civilised layer to the primitive man beneath.

She felt a thrill of fear shot through with a wild surge of elation, and knew she'd scored the equivalent of an own goal, because she was feeling pretty primitive herself. For a second she thought he was going to kiss her, waited for it with a thumping, hopeful heart.

Then he was in control again and she realised to her shame that she was not. She watched his expression close down, saw the flame die from his eyes as they returned to neutral, and heard with disbelieving ears the calmness with which he said, 'I'm sorry. I never meant to get— physical.'

He made the word sound like an affliction, but perhaps that was only where she was concerned. She felt humiliated, although that was nothing to the deeper humiliation of knowing he must have read the naked desire in her eyes as surely as she'd read it in his.

The difference was that he'd fought and controlled himself, while she'd had no thought for anything but surrender. He mustn't guess that. She'd die of shame. To salvage what she could of her pride, she said, as soon as she could trust her voice, 'I know. We just seem to bring out the worst in each other. It happens sometimes.'

It had never happened to her before, although there was no way he could know that. She wished he would go away so she could get herself together. At the same time, she wished he would never go away. She was shattered. Unlike him, she didn't have two skins. She couldn't step from one to the other with ease.

'Did I hurt you?' he asked.

She could feel the imprint of his fingers on her shoulders so positively it was hard to believe they weren't still there. Her sweater hid the marks, but it was up to her to hide the sensations he'd aroused. 'That's all right,' she replied as lightly as she could, 'I don't bruise easily.'

'I can imagine,' he said drily.

The implication took Elisa's breath away, and she gasped, 'You mean I look the type that's used to being pulled about by men? In fact——' and her anger grew as she followed the implication through '—that's been your attitude all along. You took me for a tramp from the start. You've got a colossal nerve! Just what is it about me that gets right up your nose? I've got a right to know.'

He wasn't going to tell her. She knew that the moment he turned away and stared up at the hills behind the taverna. 'It's no good looking for inspiration up there,' she snapped. 'I'm down here and I'm only interested in the truth.'

He turned back. 'Let's get back to the point. We've strayed enough from it.'

'That's not my fault,' she broke in.

She might just as well have held her breath, for he continued inexorably, 'When you picked up my daughter this morning she was on the point of taking a short cut through the olive groves to the sea. All she would have found was another hill, and another. Those paths wander all over the place. She would have been well and truly lost and I wouldn't have known where to start looking for her. You did me a good service, for which I'd like you to dine with me, and I'm not in the habit of dining with tramps. Does that satisfy you?'

'No, it doesn't, and I'm not in the habit of dining with married men, either.'

'I'm not married.'

Her treacherous heart did a somersault and then fell flat. It wasn't better that he was free, it was worse. She was vulnerable rebound material. The crazy way her emotions reacted to him was proof of that, and she sensed that underneath this veneer of courtesy he still distrusted her as much as she distrusted him.

That was no basis for a relationship, even if he was offering one, which she doubted. She wasn't interested in physical thrills. She wanted an enduring relationship—when she was ready—with an uncomplicated, loving man. Sinclair was neither, but there must be just such a man somewhere. The trick was not to get sidetracked before she found him.

Then she found herself wondering whether he was in the same situation she was. He had a child but he wasn't married. There had to be a trauma somewhere. Death or divorce, she didn't know, but he was too physical a man to be happy living alone. She'd discovered that fast enough and she hadn't even been trying.

So perhaps...just perhaps...Sinclair was looking for somebody, too, but this time that 'somebody' had to be exactly right. No more mistakes, no more being ground up in the emotional mill. Or that 'somebody' had to be as perfect as the wife she was meant to replace, if it was that kind of tragedy.

Either way she, Elisa, didn't fit the bill. That would account for his antagonism. If he was attracted to her against his will, then naturally she had to be choked off before she became a hazard. That was precisely the way she felt about him.

They might be compatible physically, but they were experienced enough to know that in every other way they were misfits. She wished she could tell him not to worry, they were both in the same boat and she had no intention of rocking it—always assuming she was right about him, of course.

If she wasn't, she didn't think she was far out. In fact, she was so convinced she'd found the answer to his hostility that she felt a flash of fellow feeling for him. It killed her own hostility stone dead.

She said quietly, 'It doesn't matter whether you're married or not. I'm afraid that was just my turn to be a pompous ass. Frankly, I lost my temper and my sense with it. I suppose that also makes it my turn to apologise.'

She glanced up at him. He was looking at her intently, too intently for comfort, but not for the life of her could she read his expression. She cleared her throat, a sign of nervousness she could have done without, then went on firmly, 'You don't have to take me to dinner, but you do have to take this back.'

She dug in her pocket for her money, counted off six one-hundred-drachma notes, and offered them to him. 'You made me feel pretty cheap when you thrust this on me. If your apologies were sincere, then you'll take it back.'

He hesitated and glanced into her clean but spartan room. 'You look as if you could do with it.'

'I'm doing very nicely, thank you, but that's not the issue. How I feel about myself is more important than how much I've got in my pocket. I'm *not* in the business of conning people.'

If he doesn't take the money, Elisa thought, I'm going to blow up again and, the way we are, he'll blow up as well.

He took the money. 'It's a clean slate then, Miss——?'

'Marshall. Elisa Marshall.'

'The Elisa part I know.' He held out his hand. 'Rafe Sinclair.'

Rafe. A clipped, cool name. It suited him. She placed her slim, tanned hand in his and watched it all but disappear as his fingers curled around it. A firm, business-like clasp, nothing personal about it. How civilised we're being, she thought. Now we've swept our emotions tidily under the carpet, we can behave as though nothing has happened or was ever likely to happen.

She should have felt triumphant. Instead she felt strangely defeated.

They should never have shaken hands. It was taking civility to the point of stupidity. Her hand felt safe in his, transmitting a feeling of belonging. The message didn't stop there, either. Her body picked it up and tried to sway towards his. Elisa had such a hard time resisting, she couldn't find the extra strength necessary to break the handclasp.

In the end, he did it for her. He said, 'Goodbye, Elisa.' He stepped back, then walked round the side of the taverna to the road.

She was left looking at the empty space where he had been. She couldn't see the higgledy-piggledy crates of empty bottles in the yard or the green of the hills beyond. She could only see him, only hear his voice.

He had called her Elisa. Not a polite 'Miss Marshall', but Elisa. Strange, that, considering how formal they'd become. Was it an acknowledgement of how things might have been between them if they were a little less cautious, a little more trusting?

Elisa sighed, a soft enough sound but it was heavy with regret. Then she locked her door and set out on her delayed pre-dinner walk. She wandered right along the beach until it curved and became even narrower, and inches of dried seaweed over scattered rocks made further progress hazardous in the fading light.

She had no option but to turn back. The lights were coming on along the beach and in the hotels and tavernas up on the coast road. A pretty sight, a wonderland in miniature, but this evening she felt no part of it.

She could have been dining with Rafe Sinclair now if she hadn't been so sensible. Or so foolish. She had done all this walking and she still wasn't sure which she had been. She only knew she felt inexpressibly sad, and that this time her sadness had nothing to do with Austyn.

It was almost as though the cure was worse than the original sickness. 'The operation was a success, but the patient died,' she said aloud, mocking herself but not feeling much inclined to laugh.

Well, she'd done one term of lovestruck mooning and she wasn't about to start another. It was time to take decisive action before any more subconscious urges led her astray again. After all, nobody knew quite as well as she did how to bite the bullet and smile as though she were enjoying it...

'Leaving?' Sue exclaimed. She was flushed and panting after another round of leading the tourists in a vigorous burst of Greek dancing. A tape of western music was playing now, and she and Rich were taking a short breather at Elisa's table. 'It's a bit sudden, isn't it?'

'That's the way I am,' Elisa said with a smile. 'As soon as I get myself comfortable some perverse streak in me gets the urge to move on. The boredom factor sets in, I suppose. No challenge.'

It wasn't true, of course, and Rich suspected it. He said, 'A couple of days ago you were full of plans for exploring the island, using this as a base. You said yourself it would be much more practical than starting up all over again in different resorts. What happened?'

Rafe Sinclair happened, Elisa thought, but she couldn't tell him that. Instead she said lamely, 'I'm restless. Maybe I'm turning into a real vagabond.'

Somebody at another table raised a hand for service. Sue stood up. 'I'll get it.'

When she'd gone, Rich murmured, 'You're running again. What from?'

Elisa groaned. 'Oh, no, Rich, no more analysing for your thesis, please! It may be close to your heart, but it's driving me up the wall.'

'You mean I'm a boring part of a boring scene?'

She covered his hand with hers for a brief, affectionate second. 'I don't mean that, idiot! I have three months left of being a free spirit and I intend to make the most of it, that's all.'

'Ah, yes, the remainder of your "year of freedom". I never really believed what you told me, but you already know that.'

Elisa was silent. She'd told Rich that, after the steady slog of school, college and job experience, she felt she'd earned a year of freedom before settling down for a further slog of building a career or marrying and raising a family, if not both. It had sounded convincing enough to her, but Rich wasn't an easy man to fool. Too many brains and too much sensitivity.

She wondered if, under his chilly exterior, Rafe Sinclair had any sensitivity. A man was a bit of a pain without it. Damn, she was thinking of him again. Perhaps moving to another resort wasn't enough. Perhaps she should get off the island altogether.

Rich was going on, 'A lot of seasonal workers have given me more or less the same reason, yet somehow, with you, it never rang true. You're a beautiful, well-qualified woman. You could get a good job anywhere without travelling with a pack on your back.'

'You're forgetting the allure of irresponsibility,' she told him lightly.

'I don't think that's a factor with you. You haven't been truthful, so you have something to hide. That's a simple enough deduction. If you were looking for something—novelty, excitement, adventure, romance—you wouldn't have anything to hide, so the obvious conclusion is that you're running away from something you don't want to talk about. That's why I'm unhappy with your case history. It isn't honest.'

'Thank you, Sherlock Kenwood,' Elisa said drily. 'If you don't like my case history, drop it.'

'If I only used straightforward stuff, my thesis would be dull and inaccurate. It's the complexity of motive that makes it fascinating and human. You were happy in your little niche here. What jolted you out of it?'

'Now you *are* becoming boring, Rich. Drop it, will you?'

He looked at her a long time. There were a lot of things he wanted to say, but by a supreme effort of will he bit them back. Instead he said, 'All right, mystery lady, I'll let you off the hook. In return, come back and see me before you leave Corfu. Maybe we can talk some more then.'

Elisa put her hand over his again and, this time, left it there. 'Rich, you're a smashing man.'

'But not *your* man, eh? Shame about that.' Then he shrugged and smiled. 'What time are you leaving tomorrow?'

'Around midday. I have a lot of people to say cheerio to first, and I won't leave the island without looking you up, Rich. Promise.'

'Fair enough.' He stood up. 'We'll have a farewell drink later when most of the crowd's gone and we're down to the tail-enders. Is that all right, or do you want an early night?'

'It's fine with me.' The last thing Elisa wanted was to go to bed until she was exhausted enough to be certain of sleeping. She didn't want to spend half the night haunted by Austyn and the other half haunted by Rafe. She checked her thoughts hurriedly. She was familiarising Sinclair, using his first name. She mustn't do that. He was nothing but a substitute for Austyn, and since when had she been interested in anything less than the real thing?

Sue came back as Rich left, and sat down to finish her lemonade. She said hesitantly, 'Elisa, if you're going off just like that, does it mean there's nothing special between you and Rich?'

'I like to think we're special friends. If you mean involved—no, there's nothing like that between us.'

'Great,' Sue responded naïvely. 'I think he's terrific, only he's never really noticed me. Maybe I should make myself more interesting for his thesis, lead him up the garden path a bit.'

'So long as you don't mind ending up in the potting shed... He's a man as well as an academic, remember.'

'I'm not likely to forget.' Sue grinned, then went on, 'Elisa, is your going away anything to do with the man who was here asking for you earlier on this evening? He said his name was Sinclair and he wanted to thank you for looking after his daughter, or some such thing. I know I shouldn't have told him where you lived, but he was really terrific, too, the type any girl would be glad to have knocking on her door.'

So that's how Rafe had found her. She should have guessed. 'It was a bit of a risk, Sue. He might have been a weirdo—and you'll have to stop falling for every good-looking fellow you see.'

'I'm not interested in him. I thought you might be. It seemed a good idea to help things along a bit because, well, that would have left Rich in the clear, wouldn't it? It was only afterwards I realised I wasn't doing you any favours because he must be married. I'm sorry about that.'

'He's not married,' Elisa replied evenly, 'not any more, and he only wanted to thank me for stopping his little girl from getting lost. That's all there was to it.' Was it? she wondered. Was that really all?

'Then you're not leaving because of him. Great! I thought you might have been trying to disentangle yourself from a married man, and I'd put my foot in it. Er—don't tell Rich what I did, will you? I don't want him to think I'm a scheming bitch, even if I am.'

'Are you kidding?' Elisa mocked. 'I'm the last one to put any false ideas in his head about me. I don't want any lectures. I've had enough hassle from him already over my wretched case history.'

How fortunate, she thought, that Sue was so much easier to deceive than Rich. Already the merry brown eyes were gleaming as the little brunette repeated,

'Hassle. If that's that it takes to interest him, that's what he'll get from me.'

'And may you both live happily ever after,' Elisa replied with a flippancy she was far from feeling. She envied Sue her ability to fall in and out of love without effort or heartbreak. Women like herself, who didn't fall easily, were so much more vulnerable when they did.

Somebody once wrote that everyone had three loves—a first love, a last love and a lost love. With Austyn she'd thought she'd had all three in one. Now she'd met Sinclair she wasn't so sure, but there was never any reassurance in uncertainty. She wasn't running for nothing...

CHAPTER FOUR

ELISA didn't see the Land Rover, or Rafe watching her as he waited for the traffic snarl-up to sort itself out. She was standing by the roadside, waiting to flag down the next bus south. Her heavy backpack was propped against the low wall of a taverna and her face was cupped in Rich's hands.

'You've got your list of contacts,' he said for the umpteenth time since insisting on taking a few minutes off from the café to carry her backpack up to the road.

'In my pocket,' Elisa replied, also for the umpteenth time, and patting her jeans' pocket as though that would reassure him. 'Don't worry. If things don't work out I can always come back.'

She thought she'd get that in before he did, and wished the bus would come along because she hated protracted farewells. The trouble was, on Corfu, timetables existed to be ignored. The bus might be on time, it might be ten minutes early or twenty minutes late. There was never any telling, and she didn't want Rich to get heavy...

He kissed her forehead. 'Right, then, take care.'

'I will.'

Still he lingered, moving his hands to her shoulders and saying, 'I'd like to kiss you on the lips. Just once. To see what it's like.'

Fond of him, she raised her face. He kissed her, then said, 'Hm. Friendly but not frantic.'

'That's me in a nutshell. You'd better get back to work, Rich. I don't want you getting in a row over me. The bus might be ages yet.'

He nodded and stepped back. 'Be seeing you, then.'

'Be seeing you.' She watched him walk away and waved back when he raised a hand in half salute before turning down a narrow path between shops to take a short-cut to the beach.

The sun was fierce and Elisa tipped her straw hat forward over her eyes. Funny, Rich was the sort of man she meant to marry some day, but never once had she felt in the slightest danger of falling in love with him. I must like making things hard for myself, she thought, slapping away a fly that settled on her cheek, and sitting down on the taverna wall for what might be a long wait.

She looked not very hopefully for the bus, and noticed for the first time that the traffic wasn't moving. A battered Volkswagen, double-parked, had effectively blocked both lanes and the nearest vehicle on her side was a Land Rover. The next second she was looking into Rafe Sinclair's eyes. He beckoned.

She hastily looked away. It was a silly, schoolgirlish reaction, made unthinkingly. She had to keep up the pretence or look even more foolish. As the traffic began to move she became absorbed in contemplating the different greens of the tree-studded hills rising sharply behind the hotels, waiting for the Land Rover to pass by.

It stopped right in front of her. All the windows were open and Rafe sat there, drumming his fingers on the steering wheel. She had to look at him and he said, 'Put your luggage in the back and jump in.'

No smile, no greeting, just the curt command. Elisa, ever a social creature, couldn't react the same way. She replied breezily, 'Thanks all the same, but no need to bother. The bus is just about due.'

He didn't argue. He just got out, came round to open the rear door, and lifted her baggage in. Then he opened the front door and looked at her. She wondered wildly if he was going to lift her in, too. Presumably he wasn't working today, because he was wearing shorts and an open-necked shirt with the sleeves rolled up.

He was roughly the same height and physique as Rich, but Rich didn't overpower her in such a physical, leg-weakening way. She looked at his tanned and muscular arms and legs, and clung to the wall as though it was her last defence. 'What are you waiting for?' he asked.

Elisa opened her mouth to argue, but the drivers behind, having endured one hold-up patiently, reacted angrily to a second. There was a sudden blast of horns. She panicked, jumped off the wall and into the car. Rafe shut the door on her, got into the driver's seat and drove off.

'I think I've been kidnapped.' Elisa meant to make it sound like a joke, but it came out more of a grumble. She wished she could treat him like any other man. This terrible awareness of him made her as fluttery as a thirteen-year-old with a first-ever crush.

'What do you think I am? A white slaver?' he asked, weaving in and out of the traffic on this congested stretch of road.

'You could be, for all I know.' It was another joke that fell flat. She tried to remind herself they'd parted amicably enough. There wasn't the slightest reason for her to be nervous—and yet she was more skittish than the proverbial cat on the hot tin roof.

It was his closeness, his bare arms and legs, the over-whelming physical appeal of him. She was terrified of touching him, yet wanted to more than anything in the world. She sat rigidly, staring straight ahead through the windscreen, fearful her eyes or her hands would stray his way if she relaxed for a moment.

It was like being with Austyn all over again, only Austyn had known and felt the same way. They had been *simpatico*. With Rafe there was the antagonism, the scarcely suppressed distrust, and only the mindless re-action of body chemicals to bind them together. If they permitted it—which they would not. Even the fervency with which she denied such a possibility had its fright-ening aspect.

It suggested that it wasn't Rafe she distrusted, it was herself.

'Where are you going?' he asked.

'I don't know,' she replied distractedly, then ex-plained. 'Not exactly, that is. I was going to ride the bus as far as Kavos if I didn't like the look of any place before then. I'm due to meet up with my travelling partner again in Athens in a fortnight, and I want to see as much of Corfu as I can in the meantime.'

'Does your partner back there know about the one in Athens?' he asked drily.

'What partner?' She was relaxing a little bit now and she turned to look at him.

She saw his eyebrows rise as he asked, 'Are there so many?'

She realised he must have seen Rich kissing her goodbye and said, 'Oh, you mean Rich. He's just a friend.' She couldn't really blame him for jumping to the wrong conclusion. The first time he'd seen her she'd been larking about on the beach with Rich. She cleared up any remaining misunderstanding by adding, 'My partner's a girl, another teacher like me. She's teaching English for a month at an international school in Athens.'

Rafe's blue eyes met hers briefly before he looked back at the road. 'Your boyfriend didn't look happy to see you go, but I suppose he didn't have much choice.'

'No, he didn't, because he's not my boyfriend. In any case, I'll look him up before I leave the island,' Elisa replied, beginning to feel resentful.

'That will be something for him to look forward to.'

He sounded so sarcastic, her resentment edged towards anger. 'Whatever, it's no business of yours. Look, your turnoff's coming up. Drop me at this garage. I can wait for the bus there. I don't want to be left in the middle of nowhere like a hitch-hiker.'

Her eyes widened when he drove straight past the garage and the turn-off. 'Kavos is right down south, miles out of your way. You don't have to take me there.'

'I'm not,' he replied coolly.

'Then where are we going?'

'Eventually, home.'

'Home? Whose home?'

'Mine. You wanted to be kidnapped, didn't you?'

'No, I didn't. Rafe, this isn't funny.' It was the first time she'd used his name, but she was too alarmed to notice it.

He noticed it, though, and became just as personal. 'Relax, Elisa. You like excitement, don't you? Adventure, the unexpected, close encounters with strange men?' His hand came over and stroked her thigh.

Elisa jumped like a startled hare and knocked his hand away. Then she dived for the door-handle and scrambled to get out. He leaned across her and grabbed the door as he slammed on the brakes. The Land Rover skidded on loose gravel, then steadied and came to a halt.

His arm was still across her, holding her in and the door shut. She shrank away from him but he said calmly, 'Sorry about that. I had to be certain you were a decent girl before I hired you. Some of the summer workers are no better than alley cats.'

'H-hired me?' she stuttered, only slowly coming out of her panic.

He took his arm away, settled back in the driving seat and started up the engine. 'I'll explain everything over lunch. If you don't want to work for me, I'll take you to Kavos or anywhere else you want to go. Either way, you're safe with me. Am I forgiven?'

Elisa didn't know what to say. Normally a fast thinker, he had a habit of paralysing her brain. Apparently he took her forgiveness for granted because he drove off with her. When she eventually found her voice, she concentrated on essentials, telling him flatly, 'I don't want to be hired.'

'You'll have a regular salary and living conditions a darned sight better than you're used to,' he replied, as though she didn't know what was good for her. 'Hold on.'

The warning was just in time as he turned down a pot-holed track, densely hedged with myrtles. Startled blackbirds fled with shrill, indignant cries, and Elisa would have followed them if she'd had half a chance. She hung on for dear life as the Land Rover bucked and jolted like a rodeo horse, gasping, 'What happens if we meet a car coming the other way?'

'I'll probably swear.'

'I already am.'

He snatched a second to look at her. Elisa thought she saw amusement in his eyes. She took a chance and smiled. He smiled back. She felt a glow of warmth—

and shyness—and looked hastily back at the track. She was more confused than ever.

For a moment, just a fleeting moment, she felt they'd established real contact at last. Nothing to do with the flesh, more to do with the spirit. The track evened out, and with it her emotions. She no longer felt panic of any kind. Since she'd first set eyes on him he'd humiliated, enraged and scared the life out of her, then with one swift smile he'd put everything right.

It was crazy, but so was the whole situation. She couldn't analyse it, so she might as well be philosophical about it. Take it as it comes, she told herself. If he says you're safe, then you must be. After all, he seems to know exactly what he's doing, which makes one of you!

They rounded a bend and there was the sea, kingfisher-blue, flat as a mill pond, what breeze there was too faint with the heat of the sun to ruffle the surface. It made Elisa aware of how hot and dusty she felt after the bucking-bronco ride.

Rafe parked at the end of the track and switched off the engine. Elisa sat spellbound. Trees crowded down to the very edge of a crescent-shaped beach. A low-roofed peasant's house nestled among lemon trees, and a man and woman were repairing the thatch of a rickety-looking loggia built to one side of it. A few tables under the loggia were the only sign that tourists occasionally strayed into this mini paradise.

In front of the house, a rough and ready pier stretched a short way into the sea. A rowing-boat was moored to it and, a little farther out, a fishing-boat was moored. A hill rose steeply behind the lemon grove, and a glimpse of pink or white revealed where other little houses hid among the trees.

'It's perfect,' Elisa breathed. 'Absolutely unspoiled.'

'Feel flattered, I don't bring many people here.' He sounded abrupt. Elisa frowned at him. He wasn't going back to being grim and grotty, was he? If so, what was the point of bringing her here? He must have followed her line of thinking, because he said more pleasantly, 'The food's basic but good, and it's quiet. A good place for talking.'

'I had you down as a five-star man,' she murmured. 'Nothing less than the Ritz.'

'I suggest we forget wrong impressions and start again.' He came round to her side and helped her out. She was longing for a swim, but thought better of suggesting it. Rich wouldn't have hesitated to plunge in in his shorts but Rafe—well, whatever he said he was still an unknown quantity.

'One wrong impression you appear to have is that I want to work for you. I don't,' she told him as they walked towards the house. 'I like to be my own boss whenever I can.'

He didn't answer. The man and woman had stopped working and were coming towards them, beaming and with hands outstretched. They greeted Rafe like a long-lost friend, exclaiming and patting him as though they wanted to reassure themselves he was real. Elisa, whose Greek was confined to a few brief phrases, couldn't follow what was said, but Rafe spoke the language like a native.

Eventually, Rafe turned to her and said, 'Elisa, this is Spiro and Christina. I've known them since I was a little boy. It was Spiro who taught me how to swim.'

There were smiles and handshakes for her. They welcomed her in broken English and she replied in fractured Greek, which they listened to with approval rather than the amusement it deserved. Then they went into the house and Rafe led her to a table. He held a chair for her before he seated himself, and she said 'You live on Corfu, then?'

'No. My father built a villa in the hills in the fifties when Corfu was relatively undiscovered. I spent most of my school holidays here.'

'You don't like the trippers, do you?' she asked.

'Nobody likes change. I'll admit I preferred the island as it was, but the tourist industry has been good for the Corfiot economy. My father must have known what was coming when he built up in the hills. We don't see many tourists up there.'

'Except the occasional stray on a scooter,' Elisa reminded him with a smile.

'That turned out to be a good thing.'

Was it? Elisa wondered. Right now she was happy but, with Rafe Sinclair, it wasn't a feeling she expected to last. Sooner or later the antagonism would flare and they'd be at each other's throats again. She hoped it would be later, but she'd no intention of being meek to prolong the peace. She said, 'After that grope-that-wasn't-a-grope back there, Mr Sinclair seems a bit formal. Shall I call you Rafe?'

'Please do. It's important we appear friendly when you work for me.'

Elisa opened her mouth to argue, but Spiro reappeared, wearing a clean white shirt and black trousers. Rafe asked, 'What would you like to drink?'

'Something long and cool and a little bit wicked for this time of day—an ouzo and lemonade.'

'In the same glass? That's not the way the Greeks drink it.'

She smiled at his disapproval. 'I know, but I'm just a happy tripper. I have what I like, not what I *ought* to like. I left my inhibitions in England—about food and drink, I mean,' she added hastily.

'Penny tells me you're an art teacher. Are you on a working holiday, or what?'

Elisa looked away. She was going to lie to him and she couldn't do it looking into his penetrating eyes. Briefly she told him about her 'year of freedom', concluding, 'I've picked grapes in Crete, cut down bananas in Israel, taught at the school where my friend is in Athens. I've had a fortnight here so far supporting myself by sketching, and saving towards a trip we plan to make to the smaller Ionian islands and perhaps some in the Aegean as well. So, you see, I really don't need a job.'

She was about to ask what job he had in mind when Spiro brought out their drinks, a deep red wine for Rafe and her opaque mixture of ouzo and lemonade in a tall, delightfully cold glass. Elisa began to drink thirstily, then stopped. In the tourist resorts she was normally served an inch or so of ouzo topped up with lemonade. Spiro, however, appeared to believe in half and half.

The spirit was too potent to be drunk like that. She put the glass down, resolving on a cautious occasional sip with her meal. When Spiro went away, Rafe said, 'The food won't be long.'

'You've already ordered? You don't know what I like.'

'There isn't a choice.' He pointed to the jetty. 'Most of the trade comes from the small excursion boats. Time here is limited, so the demand is for drinks and quick snacks, not meals. We'll be eating what the family eats, and Christina is a very good cook.'

'Oh.' Her indignation died. 'I've told you about me, but what about you? Are you on a working holiday, or what?'

'I've been running my father's firm of consultant architects since he retired a few years ago, and expanded it into several European countries. At the moment I'm setting up a subsidiary here on Corfu. I don't like the building boom, but it's inevitable. Having a say in how the island looks in years to come seems more constructive than sitting back criticising.'

Elisa looked at the idyllic little beach and admitted, 'Change isn't always for the better. Are you an architect yourself?'

'Of course.'

There was nothing 'of course' about Rafe, Elisa thought wryly. There wasn't anything about him that she cared to take for granted! An ordinary conversation was as hazardous as crossing a minefield in the dark.

His fingernails tapped restlessly against his glass. 'I'm still recruiting Greek architects, and I'm putting the finishing touches to a design for a luxury holiday complex on the west coast. By next month the pressure will be off, but this crisis couldn't have come at a worse time—which is why I need you.'

'What crisis? I'm an artist, not an architect.'

'A professional disaster I can cope with,' he said scathingly. 'This is a personal one.'

'There's no need to snap my head off. I didn't invite myself here.'

They glared at each other. After a moment he said, 'Sorry.'

She retorted huffily, 'I'm as fed up with hearing that as you must be with saying it. Look, Rafe, whatever trouble you're in, I'm the last person to help you out of it. We're trouble enough all by ourselves. I'm surprised you don't think the same.'

'I do,' he told her grimly. 'It's Penny who thinks differently.'

'Penny? What's she got to do with this?'

'Everything. I think we could get along all right if we had to, which we do.'

It was an assumption that nettled Elisa. 'I don't *have* to do anything,' she reminded, 'and I don't intend to. We'll never get along *all right*. We have this basic problem—I speak and you don't listen. I thought you wanted me to do some sketches or something, but it doesn't really matter. I don't want to work for you in *any* capacity.'

'Not even if Penny needs you? She's under the impression you're her friend. If she's wrong, say so, and I won't bother you any more.'

'That,' Elisa told him bitterly, 'is a low blow.'

'I'll strike anywhere I have to for Penny's sake.'

His sincerity didn't add up. If he doted on the child, how come she was so repressed? Feeling she was sliding down the slippery slope to involvement, she still couldn't stop herself asking, 'Why should Penny need an almost total stranger? It doesn't say much for you as a father.'

'No, it doesn't,' he agreed harshly.

Elisa was dumbfounded. Everybody defended themselves against attack. It was human nature. Either he'd just proved he was less than human, or his arrogance was greater than even she'd imagined. Did he consider himself above mortal criticism?

Spiro gave her time to regain her scattered wits by serving lunch. It was moussaka. Nothing unusual about that, except that it had the novelty of being served in aubergine shells. Even in her confounded state, she registered that it looked and smelled delicious. There was a side salad, too, and bread. She said, 'Thank you, Spiro. It looks marvellous.'

He might not have understood her words, but there was no mistaking her smile, and he beamed before going back into the house. Automatically, she began to eat. It was the real stuff, not the bland, heated-up mixture that passed for moussaka in some restaurants.

The silence that had fallen made eating difficult. She didn't see why she should break it. One the other hand, she didn't like feeling awkward. She sneaked a glance at him and found he was looking at her. 'You don't like me, do you?' he asked.

'No, I don't.'

He nodded, as though that was understandable. 'There's no reason why you should.'

She was taken by surprise again, and knew that was why he always had the edge on her. He was about as easy to unravel as a Chinese puzzle. She told him bluntly, 'It might help if you'd stop *half* saying things and explain what this is all about.'

'I'm trying. It isn't easy.'

It was only then that it dawned on her he was feeling as awkward as she was. It simply hadn't crossed her mind that a man like Rafe Sinclair *could* feel awkward. Her ready compassion stirred, although she didn't know why because he didn't have any compassion for her. 'The beginning, as they say, is the best place to start. It saves a lot of confusion.' She hesitated, then added, 'I am a teacher. I'm used to parents with problems.'

Rafe grimaced. 'God, you sound like an agony aunt.'

'I've been sounding a lot like an aunt lately. It's very depressing,' she told him mournfully, hoping to lighten the drama a bit so they could at least talk to each other normally.

He smiled, and when Rafe Sinclair smiled he was devastatingly attractive. Elisa caught her breath. He should carry a government health warning. He was bad for her but she couldn't resist him, she just couldn't. Excitement surged over her like a wave, washing away her judgement and common sense.

Suddenly it didn't seem so inexplicable that they could be fiercely antagonistic one moment and on the verge of intimacy the next. It was the way lovers were sometimes, before they surrendered to the inevitable.

Lovers...surrender...she must be going off her head. Perhaps he was, too, because he said with a softness she wouldn't have believed him capable of, 'You're an unusual girl, Elisa.'

Her pounding heart awakened every last slumbering part of her, generating a warmth that glowed in her face, her eyes, her answering smile. It was his turn to catch his breath, and he switched off the smile she had responded to so readily.

'Unusual,' he repeated, 'and plenty of charm with it. A lethal combination.'

Only he wasn't joking. He made it sound like one of his accusations. Elisa, her emotions exposed and vulnerable, was hurt as she'd never been hurt before.

CHAPTER FIVE

ELISA was saved from making a complete fool of herself by Spiro returning to clear the table. By the time he'd served dishes of luscious wild strawberries and gone back to the house, she'd mastered the ache in her throat and surreptitiously blinked the mist from her eyes.

Stupidly, she'd lulled herself into thinking Rafe had a warm and human side. Even more stupidly, she'd responded to it. A clearer case of self-deception she couldn't imagine.

The awkwardness she'd imagined he was suffering from a few minutes ago could have been no more than his ego cracking. He was an arrogant man accustomed to ordering, not explaining. No wonder he hadn't known where to begin. Whatever crisis it was that had driven him to her, he was incapable of making a simple request for help. To him it would seem too much like grovelling.

As for his smile... Elisa flinched as the dull ache of misery within her sharpened into real pain. She didn't want to think about his smile. For all she knew, a tiger might smile like that before before it struck a helpless victim. If only she hadn't been beguiled into letting her guard slip and showing him how strongly she was attracted to him.

He must have thought she was flirting with him and needed putting in her place—wherever that place was supposed to be, she thought bitterly. How brilliantly he'd succeeded must have shown on her face. She'd been stricken, and so unexpectedly that there'd been no time for a cover-up.

Presumably this second awful silence he was permitting to lengthen between them was to let the lesson sink in, to be sure she realised how much he had the upper hand.

Or so he thought.

'To hell with it—and with you, Rafe Sinclair,' she said suddenly, pushing away her bowl of strawberries and preparing to stand up. 'As the Americans would say, I need you like I need a hole in the head. I'd like to say thanks for the lunch, but the words would choke me. Don't bother to move. I can find my own way up to the road.'

His hand shot out and seized her wrist. He used just enough pressure to keep her in her chair without hurting her, but she knew from yesterday how much strength he had in reserve if she didn't sit still. She looked pointedly from his hand to his eyes. 'One of us is living in the wrong century,' she mocked, 'and I don't think it's me.'

'You're not going anywhere until you've heard my offer,' he told her harshly. 'I'll pay you five hundred sterling for looking after Penny for two weeks. All you have to do is keep her safe and happy. I'll also cover your living and sightseeing expenses, so your salary will be pure profit. Given your style of travelling, you should be able to see all the islands you want on that.'

He must be crazy. The island was full of girls who would jump at the job for a fraction of the pay. She voiced her thoughts. 'That's not a salary. It's a bribe.'

'Yes.'

She wished he wouldn't agree with her when she wanted explanations. She fell back on the question that was beginning to haunt her. 'Why me?'

'Penny asked for you. It's the first time she's ever asked me for anything, that's why I'm not quibbling about what it costs to get you. For five hundred pounds you should be able to forget your——' for the first time he hesitated as though unsure of himself '—antipathy towards me.'

Elisa's mind was reeling. There was a lot more involved here than he was letting on. She burst out, 'It doesn't make sense. Penny's afraid to ask you even for a ride on a pedalo——'

'I know,' he broke in savagely. 'That's why it's so important she gets what she wants now.'

'Yes, but why is she afraid?'

'If you can find that out, you'll have more than earned your salary. If you need any further inducement to take the job, I can promise you won't see much of me, and once I'm home in the evening you'll be free to follow your——' again there was a hesitation, followed by a slightly contemptuous '—social life.'

Apparently convinced that she was so open to bribery she wouldn't run away, he released her wrist and put her bowl back in front of her. 'Eat your strawberries while you think about it. Christina will feel obliged to offer you something else if you don't, and she probably hasn't anything ready.'

Elisa hated pandering to his arrogance by doing as she was told, but it would be spiteful to take out her resentment on Christina. Besides, she needed time to think. The strawberries were in their natural state, without sugar or cream. She picked one up and ate it, brooding on his startling offer.

He hadn't started at the beginning, as she'd suggested. She was confused, to say the least, and her mind was teeming with questions. She asked the most obvious one. 'What's happened to Miss Tilson?'

'For a sensible woman, she's been extremely foolish. She's been suffering from a stomach upset, or so she told me, and drugging herself to kill the pain. That's how Penny managed to stray. Late last night she was doubled up, and I had to all but force her into the car to get her to the clinic in town. Appendicitis was diagnosed, and she was flown back to England by air ambulance this morning for an operation. She still didn't want to go.'

'Over-conscientious?' Elisa suggested, childishly licking her fingers after finishing the strawberries.

Rafe watched her. She looked so natural, so damned *nice*. There were times he actually believed she was, then that resist-me-if-you-can gleam would come into her eyes to remind him she was just another walking man-trap. Well, if anybody got caught this time, it wouldn't be him.

'She knows she's the lynchpin of Penny's life, the one consistent factor. She's looked after Penny since she was born, the only person who has. I'm worried how Penny will cope without her.'

Elisa frowned. 'She's got you, hasn't she?'

'Me? I'm on sufferance.' He grimaced and Elisa, taken aback, thought she'd never heard so much bitterness in anybody's voice. It didn't ease as he continued, 'I can't get close to her. She won't let me.'

Elisa felt his anguish as though it were her own. How ironic, considering he had no hesitation about hurting her whenever the mood took him. But, oh, how she wished he would stop half telling her things! As it was, she was left to guess, 'Are you saying your wife—ex-wife?—has custody of Penny and you only have her for the holidays?' She could think of no other reason why father and daughter should be estranged.

'My ex-wife did have custody. She was killed in a skiing accident three months ago.'

'Poor Penny,' Elisa gasped involuntarily, 'and now she's lost her nanny for a few weeks.'

'Precisely. That's the real tragedy. Janet Tilson has been more of a mother to her than ever Sheena was.' Again the grimace, again the bitterness. 'Now do you see why it's so important Penny gets who she wants? When I told her I'd cancel my business appointments and look after her myself, she panicked and asked for you. So you she gets.' He stood up suddenly. 'She's waiting now. If you don't want that drink, we might as well get moving.'

Elisa got to her feet, but when he came round to her side of the table and took her arm she didn't move. She was being steam-rollered into a situation more fraught than the one she'd been running away from, and she couldn't allow that. His touch, impersonal as it was, reminded her of all she had to fear.

'Look, I'm sorry for Penny——' she didn't dare tell him she was sorry for him as well '—but you're taking an awful lot for granted. I haven't said I'll work for you. In fact, I couldn't have made it plainer I don't want to.'

'You mean the bribe wasn't high enough,' he replied flatly. 'All right, name your price.'

'It isn't a question of money!' she exclaimed, exasperated.

'Then what is it a question of?' He turned her fully towards him and ran his hands slowly up her bare arms to her shoulders. Her spine retracted with pleasure, sending shivers of delight all over her body. His hands slid round to her back, pulling her against him as he explored the length of her body.

They were capable, knowing hands and they moved over her almost lazily, searching for response and arousing wave after wave of sensual pleasure. She lost her will to resist, and her mind with it. She pressed her soft curves against his lean, hard body, her head coming to rest on his shoulder, her eyes closing, her arms going around him and her hands beginning an exploration of their own.

Love and hate, she thought dreamily, opposite sides of the same coin. The coin had flipped and they'd come down in paradise.

It was only when he turned her face up to his and murmured, 'So, Elisa, I've found out what you want...' that she realised what was motivating him, and by then it was too late. His lips came down on hers and she was lost in her love and his expertise. Tears choked her because, for him, this was nothing but a manoeuvre to get his own way. There was nothing she could do about it. Everything had swung in his favour. She could only live on for the touch of his lips on hers, and die of shame because of it.

He was very thorough. It seemed an eternity before he put her away from him. Ample time for her to scale the heights and plumb the depths, and for the coin to spin again so she no longer knew which side up it was.

'Whatever it takes.' His voice broke the silence, the spell was already shattered. He seemed to be repeating a resolution for his own benefit, and he spoke so harshly that she didn't notice how unsteady his voice was. 'Come on,' he added, as though he knew he'd reduced her to a slave-like state, 'let's go.'

He was very careful not to touch her, there was no rough grabbing of her arm, but she didn't notice that, either. She was staring down at her feet, concentrating hard, willing her tears not to spill over. She caught her full lower tip between her white teeth, but still a tear rolled down her cheek, and then another.

'Stop it,' Rafe said sharply. 'I'm sick of playing games.'

Games... he thought *she* was playing games. The injustice, the indignity and the terrible sorrow of being used when she wanted to be loved checked Elisa's tears. Her indigo eyes were still swimming with them as she raised her face to his but, mercifully, none spilled over.

She slapped his handsome face so hard that, powerful as he was, he reeled back. Then she turned and walked away from him. She walked straight into the sea in her jeans and her blouse.

Rafe followed her to the water's edge. 'What the hell do you think you're doing?'

'Getting myself clean.' She plunged forward and swam out with strong clean strokes.

Her battered straw hat floated back to him. He picked it out of the sea and shook it, finding Spiro beside him as he straightened up. For a moment neither of them spoke, then Spiro said in Greek, 'It is not good to swim with a full stomach.'

'I'm watching her,' Rafe replied grimly, also in Greek.

'You should be going after her. The lady is in her clothes. They will be heavy.'

'If I go after her, she'll swim all the way to Greece. I've upset her.'

'So I can tell by your face, my friend.' The marks of Elisa's fingers stood out lividly on Rafe's tanned cheek.

Spiro smiled. 'That is good. A woman who doesn't get upset, doesn't care.'

He wasn't at all surprised when Rafe bent suddenly to unstrap his leather sandals. He cared, too, and that was also good. It was a long time since he had last brought a woman here, the one he had married, and she had been bad for him...

As Rafe straightened up and kicked off his sandals, Elisa turned and headed for the end of the beach where the Land Rover was parked. Spiro caught the relief in his voice as he said, 'She's coming in.'

He smiled. 'First she hurt you and now she will make you better. It is the way of women.'

Rafe didn't feel inclined to argue. He thrust his hands into his shorts' pocket for his money and peeled off some to give to Spiro. 'Thanks,' he said tersely, his eyes going back to Elisa, then he picked up his sandals and walked urgently towards the car.

'Bring her back another time. I like her, too,' Spiro called after him, and laughed, thinking he was witnessing nothing more than a lovers' tiff.

Rafe had never felt less like laughing. When he reached the car, he got out Elisa's pack and rested it against the back wheel. She'd need to change. She might even need to lash out at him again. He'd let her, if it would make her feel better. It might make him feel better himself...

He turned and watched her come out of the sea. She didn't look exhausted. She came out purposefully, like an angry young Amazon. Her jeans and blouse were moulded to her shapely figure. Her hair, freed by the sea from its plait, was plastered to her head and then fell in dripping rats' tails to her shoulders.

She looked beautiful, vital, wholly desirable.

Rafe wanted to look away, needed to, but couldn't. His eyes were doing what his aching body wanted, making love to her. He remembered how she'd felt in his arms, the way her soft body had moulded to his as though it were meant for no other purpose. He remembered the elation of her willingness, the sweetness of her lips, his own struggle not to surrender, which he'd so nearly lost.

She'd almost made him forget why he was kissing her. For several desperate seconds everything had become blurred, unimportant in comparison with holding her exciting body in his arms, drawing untrammelled passion from her lips.

The sensual man-trap that she was had almost snared him, and for timeless, ecstatic moments he hadn't cared. But then Penny's needs had regained ascendancy and they must, whatever the cost, remain paramount. He had come back from the brink of abandonment, shaken by how nearly he'd become a victim of his own tactics.

Elisa thought he'd been harsh with her, and he had, but it was nothing to how harsh he'd been with himself. He remembered her tears—those unexpected, unnerving tears—and was less certain which of the two of them he'd hurt the most, and would go on hurting if he had to.

Rafe's eyes were wary as she came towards him. She was ignoring him, her eyes fixed on some point over his shoulder. The heat of her rage had chilled to an implacable fury, and he knew it would spill out somewhere unless she was given time to recover herself.

He moved aside so she could reach her pack, and watched in silence while she took out a plastic bag containing a towel, then pulled out a few items of clothing. Her shoulder was almost touching him, but he might have been on the moon for all the notice she took. He looked at the tanned skin, drying rapidly in the sun, and almost envied the droplets of water that splashed on to it from her hair. How much he wanted to lower his head and lick that water away, kiss that smooth skin, taste it.

'You can change behind the car,' he said, and his voice, because he still had so much passion to hide, was harsher than ever. 'There's nobody to see and I won't look.'

She gave no indication of having heard, and strode towards the myrtle bushes lining the track up to the road. The silent treatment, he thought. Woman's ultimate weapon. It was never easy to break down. He saw her feet were bare. She must have kicked off her sandals in the sea. He thought it best to be silent himself for a while, but worry made him say, 'Watch out for snakes.'

'I'm not likely to miss you, am I?' she retorted stonily, and disappeared from his view.

Rafe leaned back against the car, a hint of respect lightening the bleakness of his eyes. She was a fighter, Elisa Marshall. And yet, unless he really had been wrong about her from the start, she shouldn't be fighting him at all. She wasn't only a fighter, she was a paradox as well.

He put Elisa's hat on the roof of the car to dry, and scowled at the bushes she had disappeared behind. Little Penny hadn't known what she'd been letting him in for when she'd asked for Elisa as a temporary nanny...

He straightened as Elisa came back on to the beach. She was wearing her cut-off shorts and a little blue suntop with narrow shoulder straps. She put the plastic bag containing her wet clothes at the base of a tree, hung her wet towel over a low branch to dry, and marched along the beach with a hairbrush in her hand.

She couldn't go far before the crescent of the beach ended in a rocky outcrop. She sat down on the last of the shingly sand and brushed her hair. Rafe stayed where he was, biding his time, watching her hair return to platinum as the sun dried it. She's ageless, he thought. With those classical features, she will always be beautiful and nobody will ever notice when that platinum hair turns to white.

The thought disturbed him on a different level from the physical havoc watching her wreaked on him. He was thinking of her in terms of the future, and she had no place in his future. It was then he realised the only way he could deal with her was to be totally bloody-minded, and he'd made a good start. It was time to capitalise on it.

He walked towards her. When he was standing over her she stood up, stalked past him and sat down again, midway between him and the car. He turned and glared at her. 'If there's one thing I detest,' he said, 'it's a woman who sulks.'

She glared rigidly out to sea. Not only was she refusing to see him, she wasn't going to hear him, either. He went and stood over her again. 'Your move,' he told her, 'if you're really into musical chairs.'

This time there was no movement at all. Rafe looked down at her consideringly, then scooped her up in his arms and carried her to his car. He expected her to start fighting and screaming and kicking, but she was too clever for that. She lay in his arms like a log, mutely resistant, saving her strength for the right moment.

He dumped her in the front passenger seat, closed the door and moved to put her pack in the back of the car, watching her like a hawk all the time. Then he moved round the car to get her plastic bag and towel. She was out of the car in a flash and sprinting towards the little house. He was after her even faster and brought her down in a rugby tackle.

Rafe picked her up and put her back in the car before she had time to get her breath back. 'We can keep this up all day if you like,' he said sardonically. 'You'll be worn out before I am.'

Elisa measured the distance from the car to the house. It wasn't so very far, if she got a good start. Rafe followed her gaze and read her mind. 'It's no good throwing yourself on Spiro's mercy. He thinks we're the best thing since Romeo and Juliet. I could chase you all over the beach and he'd only stand back and cheer.'

'You're despicable,' she fumed.

'As for Christina,' he went on imperturbably, 'she's a woman. She'll think you want to be caught. So sit still and behave yourself. I said I'd take you to Kavos if you didn't want to work for me.'

'You also said I'd be safe with you,' Elisa reminded him furiously.

'I don't remember you fighting.'

Her face flamed. Satisfied, he retrieved the rest of her belongings, put them in the back and climbed into the driver's seat. As he strapped himself in, he looked at what little he could see of her averted face. 'Put your seat-belt on,' he ordered. 'You'll have less of a bumpy ride.'

Elisa, too livid to speak, reverted to a policy of non-co-operation. She didn't move. Deliberately he reached across her for the safety strap, his shoulder touching hers, her soft hair brushing his face. She smelled fresh and clean and her hair was as sensuous as silk. He gritted his teeth, wondering how he was going to get the strap across her and keep his hands off her at the same time.

She solved the problem for him by coming back to life like a fury, pushing him away and snapping, 'All right, I'll do it. You can take me to Kavos, but that's all you can do. Don't look at me, don't talk to me, and most of all don't touch me!'

'That's suits me,' he replied, but he watched her strap herself in. The belt came across her shoulders and between her breasts before she locked it in. She wasn't wearing a bra. Rafe felt the ache in his groin and silently cursed her. He held all the aces, but she was trumping him every time. Thank God she didn't know it.

The thought crossed his mind that Sheena would have known it—depended on it—and that made Elisa different. 'Bloody hell,' he said, and started the engine.

Elisa didn't know what he was swearing about, but she didn't complain. As far as she was concerned, he was swearing for both of them. He was right about one thing, the ride back up the track wasn't so bad with the seat-belt on, perhaps partly because there were now two pairs of tanned bare legs in the car. She didn't know why that should distract her so much. It was a big car. There was no chance of them touching. It was just that she was so terribly conscious of him and that made her even more conscious of herself.

At the top of the track he turned right. Her alarm was instant. 'This isn't the way to Kavos.'

'That's right.'

'But you promised to take me to Kavos!'

'So I will,' he reaffirmed. 'Eventually.'

Elisa's alarm deepened into panic. 'What do you mean, eventually?'

'I'm not going to tell Penny you won't be her nanny,' he told her evenly. 'You are.'

Elisa's lips parted in dismay. She thought of the sorrowful little girl with huge blue eyes full of puppy-like anxiety to please, and her heart sank. She didn't think she'd be able to refuse her anything. When she found her voice, it shook with anger. 'That's the worst kind of emotional blackmail I've ever come across.'

His eyes flicked briefly to her. 'I thought it was clever.'

'You . . . you . . .' she ground out, searching for exactly the right word to describe her opinion of him.

'Bastard,' he supplied. 'I can't argue with that. The way things are, I can't promise any improvement, either.'

CHAPTER SIX

'MY GOD,' Elisa breathed as soon as she'd recovered from this latest example of his arrogance, 'no wonder your marriage broke down. You're medieval. What am I supposed to be? The little milkmaid who bobs and curtsies and does everything the master desires?'

'All you're required to do is look after my daughter for a fortnight. I don't know why you're making such a drama out of it. I'm not going to chase you up to the attic at night. This is my home I'm taking you to, not a love-nest. Penny's disturbed enough, without me introducing a string of loose women into her life.'

'I am not a loose woman!' Elisa stormed.

'I'm prepared to take your word for that,' he told her coldly, 'and you can take my word that you won't be treated as one. What you do in your own time is your business. It's only if you invite any boyfriends back you'll find out how much of a bastard I can be.'

'I don't believe any of this is happening,' she murmured wonderingly. 'I should, but I don't. You kidnap me, insult me, assault me, do every damn thing you can to force me into a job I don't want, then have the gall to behave as if *I'm* the one on sufferance. You're crazy.'

'Desperate.'

'Well, don't expect me to feel sorry for you. I'm feeling pretty desperate myself. So would you if you were shut in a car with a raving lunatic.'

He was silent for a few moments, then he said, 'You have a point.'

'Thanks very much,' she snapped. 'It's a bit late to start considering my feelings, but I appreciate the effort.'

He slammed on the brakes. Elisa's heart began a nervous tattoo, but he sat staring through the windscreen as though he'd forgotten she was there. They were high in the hills, not far from where she'd picked up Penny yesterday. The fantastically gnarled shapes of ancient olive trees pressed towards the track on either side, nets neatly spread beneath them to catch the falling crop. The slightest of breezes stirred the silver-green leaves of the trees, the only movement there was, even the birds resting during this hottest part of the day. They might have been the last people left on earth. It was an uncomfortable feeling.

Rafe moved suddenly. Elisa jumped, but he was only switching the engine off. She felt more marooned than ever, more conscious of his threatening physical presence, as the silence and heat closed in on them. He turned towards her and studied her apprehensive eyes. Then he said slowly, 'I haven't been very fair to you, have I?'

Oh, no, Elisa thought, please don't let him start being kind. Let him go on being rotten so I can hate him. I can't cope when he's being human. I just crumble...

'I meant to explain Penny's situation so you would understand properly why I need you, but when it came to it, I couldn't. It's not easy to open a closed chapter in one's life,' he began, then stopped. His fingers started drumming on the steering wheel.

Elisa watched them. They were strong, well-shaped fingers. She yearned to reach across and still them but, with the tension she and Rafe generated between them, it would be easier to reach into a lion's cage than touch him voluntarily. He seemed to have forgotten her again, moved into another world in which she had no place.

She wanted to bring him back to her, jealous without cause of something he wouldn't share, and she said tentatively, 'If the "chapter" refers to your marriage, surely it could never have been closed? Not with a child involved, I mean.'

'In theory, no; in practice, I was pretty well shut out, and Penny seems to want it to continue that way. She's remote and I'm—clumsy, I suppose. I can't force affection out of her. We just don't know how to be father and daughter any more.'

'That shouldn't have happened,' Elisa said, 'not if you had proper access. I deal with a lot of children from split homes at school. They usually look forward to their fathers' visits as a time to be thoroughly spoiled.'

'Penny was three when Sheena and I split up. Sheena took her to the States. I rarely had the chance to see Penny. She was turned four when they returned to England, and the damage was done. She just couldn't accept me as a father again. Possibly there were so many of her mother's boyfriends in and out of her life, she got confused—or Sheena deliberately turned her against me.'

'Surely she wouldn't have been that spiteful?'

'Sheena?' His lips twisted. 'She took Penny in the first place to spite me. She never wanted her, but she knew I did. Penny was just a weapon, something to be dumped with Janet Tilson when her usefulness was over, while she went swanning off with other men. My mistake was divorcing her before she was ready to go. That fractured her belief that she was an irresistible woman, and she struck back through Penny.'

His bitterness chilled Elisa. 'You're not sorry she's dead, are you?'

'You've seen Penny. Would you be sorry if she were your child? Sheena's responsible for the way she is, and she wouldn't have let her go. She knew I was burning up over what was happening to Penny, just as she knew I was helpless to do anything about it. That was my punishment for not staying in love with her. Now she's gone, I'm not shedding any crocodile tears. I'm just grateful there's time to turn Penny back into a normal child. A few more years and——' He shrugged.

'You're bitter,' Elisa began hesitantly, 'and bitterness can warp the judgement. You want a target, and that doesn't make you all that much better than Sheena, does it? I'm not even sure you've got the right one. You said yourself it's Janet Tilson who's brought Penny up.'

'I've thought of that, but it's Janet Penny turns to as a refuge, not me. She needs her, if nothing else. I'm beginning to wonder if Penny is like her mother, incapable of love for anybody but herself. All I'm certain of is, it will be a fortnight before I can get a reliable replacement from England, and in the meantime she doesn't want me to look after her. She wants you.'

Elisa looked at his fingers still restlessly drumming on the steering wheel, and couldn't stop herself being swamped with compassion. She sighed and said, 'I can imagine how you feel.'

He rounded on her, his eyes as cold as chips of ice. 'No, you can't,' he told her savagely. 'I know exactly why Penny wants you. You remind her of her mother. Just make damned sure you don't behave like her while you're in my house, that's all.'

He switched on the engine, slammed into gear and drove on.

'Oh, that's great! Your family is in a mess and it's all my fault!' Elisa exclaimed, spilling out a bitterness that mocked his own. 'Thanks for being so *fair* and explaining it all, otherwise I might have carried on making a fuss. Now I realise *I'm* the guilty party, naturally I'll try to behave myself. In my spare time I'll do my best to come to terms with my persecution complex!'

He stopped the car again, put his hand under her chin and turned her face to his, looking long and hard into her blazingly indignant eyes. 'Elisa,' he said finally, 'you're quite a girl.'

'Drop dead,' she snarled.

He released her and drove on. 'Don't spoil a magnificent performance by becoming petty.'

Elisa gave up. All his words got through to her, and all hers bounced straight off him. He was an impossible man. Bitter, twisted and, now and again, bloody magnificent himself.

He swung the car off the dirt road on to a track, and began a winding climb through an olive grove. They passed a small white-painted farmhouse with a motley collection of ramshackle outbuildings, and he said, 'That's where Spiro and Maria Pappadoukalis live with their children Angelo and Athene. Maria comes up to act as housekeeper and cook, if necessary, although we mostly eat out. On Saturday she and Athene give the house a thorough clean, so we usually make ourselves scarce. You won't find yourself burdened with any domestic duties, apart from breakfast.'

'I'm not going to be burdened with anything,' she told him grimly. 'I'll say hello to Penny and explain myself why I can't look after her. I'll tell her my holiday here is over and I have to move on.'

He didn't answer. She looked at him suspiciously. 'I hope your box of tricks is empty. If Penny's disturbed, the last thing she needs is us quarrelling in front of her.'

'I knew you'd be reasonable once I got you to Penny,' he replied, and she could cheerfully have strangled him, but he was nodding ahead. 'There it is.'

From what Rafe had said the house was about thirty years old, but the design had been freely borrowed from classical Greek architecture, giving it a timeless quality. It was two-storeyed, and reminded Elisa of nothing so much as a miniature temple, scaled down to perfect proportions and domesticated. The pillars supporting the veranda at the front extended on either side of the house to form loggias, under which white-painted wrought-iron garden furniture nestled and large flower-filled pottery urns made bold splashes of colour.

Elisa fell in love with it—almost. What jarred on her was that it was painted pink. As Rafe parked, she said, 'It's beautiful, but it should be white.'

'It was until Sheena and I honeymooned here. Pink was her favourite colour.'

He must have been passionately in love with her, she thought, to spoil the effect of his lovely house just to please her. Perhaps he still was, in spite of all he said, and although she was lost to him forever. He had left the house pink.

She was disturbed. Almost jealous. She was discovering a dark side of herself she hadn't known existed. She couldn't leave well alone, and when he got out of the car and came round to her side, she said, 'You're an architect, I'm an artist, we both know the house is crying out to be white. Why haven't you changed it back?'

'It's been rented out for summer lets. I haven't been back for four years.' He looked at her searchingly, as if surprised by her interest. Elisa avoided his eyes, afraid of what he might read in them. She mustn't become as involved with the house as she'd become with the man. It would be like another tentacle reaching out to trap her.

When Rafe opened the back door and hauled out her pack, she said sharply, 'I don't need that. I'm not stopping.'

'We'll see.' He thrust the plastic bag containing her wet clothes into her hand, took her arm and propelled her towards the front door, carrying the pack himself. As they passed between the slender columns of the veranda, the front door opened. A plump middle-aged woman with a strongly boned face and ready smile emerged and came towards them.

'Maria, or Mrs Pappas as Penny calls her,' Rafe explained. 'She's been keeping an eye on Penny for me while I looked for you. She speaks very little English, which makes her unsuitable as a constant companion just now. I need somebody Penny can communicate with.'

Elisa smiled and greeted the woman, who was smiling and chattering and obviously welcoming her profusely into the house. She thinks I'm stopping, too, she thought with dismay. I'm getting in deeper and deeper, just as Rafe planned.

Mrs Pappas insisted on taking her plastic bag, and Elisa shot a kindling glance at Rafe. 'You're doing your best to make it impossible for me, aren't you?'

'Yes.' He was looking beyond Mrs Pappas. Penny stood in the doorway. She was dressed, as she had been on the two previous occasions Elisa had seen her, in an expensive frock with long sleeves and a crisp white collar. She came forward with a curious mixture of hesitancy and eagerness.

'Hello, Daddy,' she said. 'You've been a long time.'

'Hello, Penny. It took me a while to find Elisa, but here she is.'

'Yes,' the child answered seriously, then turned to Elisa. 'Hello. I'm so pleased you could come.'

Definitely six years old going on sixty, Elisa thought. Such a polite welcome, no sign of childish joy at getting what she wanted; but Penny was going on, 'I'll take you up to your room. I'm sure you'll be very comfortable. It's right next to mine. Mrs Pappas has made up the bed and I've collected some flowers.'

Elisa cast a despairing look at Rafe's unsympathetic face and swallowed. No use looking for any help there. He'd won every round so far, and now he was within an ace of winning the battle. 'Penny,' she said gently, 'the reason Daddy took so long to find me was because I've finished my holiday here and I was travelling on to somewhere else.'

'Oh.' Penny's passive face became anxious. 'Can't you stay?'

'I'm afraid not.' She winced as Rafe's clasp on her arm tightened like a vice. She looked at him and read murder in his eyes. But he couldn't, he really couldn't, have expected to get away with all this.

Penny's face went blank again. She said, as politely as ever, 'I see. Thank you for coming to see me.' If she'd left it at that, Elisa could have forced herself to walk away, but Penny bowed her head and mumbled, 'I'm sorry if I've been a nuisance.'

It was her docility, her utter lack of protest, that touched Elisa's heart. She looked down at the fair curls and found herself saying, 'On the other hand, now I've seen what a lovely place this is, I don't think I have to move on. I could have a very nice holiday here. We both could, with the beach and pedalos not very far away.'

Penny's head shot up, her eyes filling with excitement. 'Truly? Honestly and truly?'

It was the first time Elisa had heard her sound like a child. She felt Rafe's grip loosen on her arm as she smiled and repeated, 'Honestly and truly. How about showing me my room? I want to see those flowers you've picked for me.'

'They keep flopping. I'll just see if they're still all right first,' Penny exclaimed, and dashed into the house. Mrs Pappas followed her, beaming and beckoning, but Elisa chose to say where she was for the moment.

'Go on, gloat,' she told Rafe. 'It worked out just as you knew it would—heads you win, tails I lose.'

But he was looking after Penny. Almost to himself, he said, 'She ran, and I've only ever seen her walk everywhere. It's one of the things that's so unnatural about her.' He seemed to become aware he had been spoken to, and looked at Elisa. 'Did you say something?'

'Nothing that would have changed anything,' she replied despondently. She didn't exist as a person in her own right as far as he was concerned. She was just a means to an end in the reclaiming of his daughter. She tried to bolster her flagging spirits by reminding herself she was staying for Penny's sake, not his. She needed all the morale boosting she could get, which was why it didn't occur to her the two were indivisible.

He had heard her previous remark, though, and as it penetrated his consciousness he recalled, 'Gloat? I'm not gloating. I'm too damned grateful for that.'

And so you should be, she thought resentfully, but knew immediately it wasn't his gratitude she wanted. 'You don't have to be grateful. You're paying me well, remember.'

'Yes, but that was never a factor, was it?' His face was inscrutable as he gazed down at her, and she was taken by surprise as he held out his hand. 'Shake on a new beginning, Elisa?'

Grudgingly she put her hand in his, but she grumbled, 'That's about the third one. By tonight we'll probably be up to the tenth.'

'No, we won't. We'll get on better now. You keep Penny happy, I'll stay out of your hair. It will because we both have the same objective.'

He sounded so sure of himself, but then he always was. She was the one full of doubts, and she was reminded of the worst of them when he once more took her arm and steered her towards the door. She couldn't stop herself responding to his touch, whether it was gentle or cruel, and she was already beginning to feel the strain of hiding her reaction from him. What would she be like after a fortnight of close proximity?

It had been bad enough with Austyn, but she hadn't had to hide her feelings from him, only from those who might be watching, and they'd both had to do that. They'd been *together* in an impossible situation. With Rafe it was entirely different. She was on her own...and she distrusted the emotion he aroused in her.

He'd given her every reason to loathe, not love him. He'd bruised her body, her pride, her own image of herself. If she were a hopelessly romantic girl like Sue, always falling in love with somebody, it would be understandable—but she wasn't. She was nearly twenty-six and she'd only fallen passionately in love once; that it could happen again only nine months later was inconceivable. It was even more inconceivable that she could have fallen for such an unlikable man.

If it was love for its own sake she wanted, why hadn't she fallen for Rich? He had given her every opportunity, and he was so *suitable*. Why had she fallen for Rafe? She wasn't perverse enough to *enjoy* suffering, for heaven's sake!

No, the truth was as obvious as ever. Rafe had made such a positive impact on her because his contemptuous attitude had challenged all her feminine instincts, awakening her, and opening up a channel through which her frustrated love for Austyn could flow.

It had to be that. *She couldn't possibly love Rafe Sinclair himself!*

Resisting Austyn had worn her down, which was why she was so frightened now. She didn't want to become a pushover for the wrong man. Rafe, bulldozing towards his own objective, neither knew nor cared what he was doing to her—and she had to share a house with him for a fortnight!

'Oh, God...' she groaned, and was horrified she'd spoken aloud.

'What's the matter?' They were in a large flagstoned hall. Rafe was leading her towards the stairs at one side when he paused to frown at her.

'I—I'm not at all sure this is going to work out.' She sounded so lame, and her throat was so dry. She'd let one particularly objectionable man reduce her to this inarticulate and pitiful state. Perhaps she deserved all she got. She licked her lips and continued more positively, 'I might do more harm than good. Penny might need specialist help.'

'I've had it, and it hasn't worked. I was told she needed time to recover from the trauma of Sheena's death, although she rarely saw her mother. Well, she's had time, but she's getting worse not better. I was told she should play with other children but she won't, and I can't see that forcing her is going to help. All that's happened is that her rejection of me has become more complete and her dependence on Janet Tilson more total. Or so I thought, until she asked for you. It was an impulsive, instinctive request, and I'm backing it. The responsibility isn't yours, so you can stop worrying about it.'

When Elisa didn't answer, he added, 'I know it's a gamble, if that's what you're bothered about—but it's a gamble in which I'm taking all the risks.'

She couldn't tell him how wrong he was. She could only follow him tamely up the stairs feeling more personally at risk than she'd ever been in her entire life. A sound in the hall below made her glance back down. It was Mrs Pappas reappearing to shut the front door. That seemed to make it final, somehow.

Like it or not, she'd become part of Rafe Sinclair's uneasy household.

CHAPTER SEVEN

WITHIN four days Elisa had stopped dreading each new encounter with Rafe and was beginning to treasure what little time they spent together. They met at breakfast with an intimacy that would have been overpowering if it hadn't been for Penny's presence. As it was, they seemed like any other family getting ready to start the day.

Elisa knew now what Rafe liked to eat and how he liked it cooked, when he liked to talk and when he liked to be quiet. She also knew what he looked like before he shaved, and he knew how she looked with tousled hair scuffed up in a ponytail while she clattered about the kitchen preparing to get him off to work. She was not the most domesticated of creatures, and he wasn't a man who was used to helping out. Breakfast was a chaotic hit-and-miss affair but, strangely, it was fun.

They made, consciously and unconsciously, all those little concessions necessary to keep an ill-assorted man and woman living in harmony. It hadn't been as impossible as Elisa had feared. Familiarity had lowered the barriers, enabling them to behave as they'd never managed before—naturally. The sexual tension that might have spoiled all this was dealt with in a very English way. It was ignored.

That they'd come so far towards an amicable relationship in such a short time was largely due to Elisa. Locked into Rafe's life against her will, the need to survive had forced her to stop fighting the situation and figure out the best way to cope with it.

In fact, there was only one way. She didn't know how to be Rafe's employee or Penny's nanny, so she could only be herself. In a domestic setting that meant not standing on ceremony with either of them. She behaved exactly as she did in her own home with her own family, and it worked. It took Rafe and Penny longer to respond as naturally, but not all that much longer.

Rafe wasn't exactly a changed man—she still caught him looking at her with that coldly assessing expression sometimes—but he was always reasonable, and he had certainly made things as easy for her as he could. He'd given her the keys to the car he'd hired for Janet Tilson for the season, and the key to the drawer in his study where he kept a sum of money for the daily expenses of looking after Penny.

Apart from breakfast, the only other occasion Elisa could be sure of spending some time with him was in the evening before Penny went to bed. Afterwards, he disappeared into his study and stayed there. She wondered wistfully whether this was his way of keeping his promise to 'stay out of her hair', or whether he frankly preferred his own company to hers.

Either way, she was about to change the household routine. After four days of following Janet Tilson's system, she felt confident enough to impose her own, for the change in Penny had been remarkable.

Elisa hadn't had to winkle her out of her shell, Penny had all but fallen out of it. They'd become, as Elisa laughingly put it, beach bums. They motored around the island from resort to resort, swimming, building sandcastles, playing ball, taking out pedalos or joining boat excursions.

Heavy inroads had been made on the money in the 'daily expenses' drawer, far more than Janet ever made,

Elisa suspected. She left a careful account of how the money was spent and Rafe never quibbled. He just kept the amount topped up. In that respect, Elisa often thought wryly, he'd be a nice sort of husband to have.

Initially she'd spent a fair bit on clothes for Penny. An inspection of her wardrobe had revealed too many prissy frocks and shiny shoes, and hardly any play clothes or sandals. A shopping expedition had righted the balance, and now Penny, to her delight, was dressed like a mini Elisa, in jeans and loose sweaters when the weather was capricious, and shorts and brief tops when the sun shone.

Knowing how Penny never asked for anything, Elisa asked if there was anything else she'd like. 'A hat like yours,' Penny had replied with a promptness that was a good sign.

They bought one, but Penny said, 'It's too smart. It's not like yours.'

'I can soon fix that.' Elisa unpicked the rim, frayed the straw, and sat on it. 'This is called instant ageing. Mine took months to get so battered.' She felt a pang as she remembered the day Rafe fished her hat out of the sea...the day she'd learned it really was possible to love and hate a man at one and the same time.

When Penny got her hat back, she was pleased but apprehensive. 'Gosh, won't Daddy be cross?'

'He'll probably want one like it,' Elisa replied, sorry to see her slipping back into anxiety. 'You'll have to show him how it's done.'

Penny giggled. Delighted, Elisa giggled with her, and Penny sat on the hat herself. Her anxiety surfaced again when they were driving home, and she said, 'I thought Daddies didn't like things being spoilt.'

'Are you still bothered about the hat? Don't be. Nobody likes people who spoil things to be spiteful. We were just—er—re-styling the hat the way you want it. There's a big difference.'

'Oh.' Penny sounded dubious, but she really loved her hat. She wore it all the time, even if it was raining, with one notable exception. When Rafe was around she hid it.

It wasn't until the fourth day that Elisa noticed her odd behaviour, and after Penny had gone to bed that evening she tackled Rafe about it. He always gave her the chance to talk privately before disappearing into his office by asking, 'Any problems?'

For the first time Elisa replied, 'Yes, if you can spare a few minutes.' The May evenings were chill up here in the hills. He didn't seem to notice it, but she was kneeling on a fur rug in the sitting-room lighting a fire. She was wearing the floppy black sweater that did such sterling service, and the best of her two pairs of jeans.

Her hair was braided into its usual plait and she sat back on her heels watching the fire, waiting for the moment she could add more coal without the burning wood collapsing into a smoking dying heap. She was pleased to have something to do, fearing their fragile relationship would break down now they were alone.

'What's happened?' he asked, surprising her by coming to sit in one of the fireside armchairs. She'd expected him to choose the settee, a safe distance away. His long legs were nearly touching her, and he was leaning forward with his arms on his knees, bringing their faces too close for comfort.

She began to feel panicky, and fiddled with the fire to hide her awareness of him. 'There are some things I need to know. Have you ever ticked off Penny for deliberately or accidentally damaging something?'

'No. She never wrecks anything the way normal children do. I wish she would. It's unnatural how careful she is.'

Elisa put some more coal on the fire, stripped off her rubber gloves and sat back on her heels. 'Why does she think she has to be so *painfully* polite and well behaved with you?'

'Because that's the proper way to treat a stranger. I told you, she won't let me get close. I don't think she wants a father. Not me, anyway.'

'It's not that. I'm the real stranger, but she's natural enough with me,' Elisa replied. 'Have you ever been so angry with her you've lost your temper and frightened her?'

'No.'

He sounded too positive to doubt, and yet she had to. She turned her face to his. It was close to sunset and the room was darkening rapidly. The fire had taken strong enough hold to cast a glow across his handsome face. In that moment, he didn't seem an unwanted substitute for Austyn. He seemed the only man in the world for her and she wanted him very much.

She said huskily, 'Are you sure? You have a hasty temper. Perhaps you don't realise how frightening you can be. You've given me a few uneasy moments.'

Rafe flung himself back in the armchair and his fingers began their familiar drumming on its arms. 'You think because I've been rough on you I've also been rough on Penny? You're wrong. I know how anxious she is, how easily intimidated. I've always treated her with kid gloves.'

Whereas you think I'm as tough as an old boot, Elisa thought wistfully. She said, 'Well, she's either terrified of you—or so anxious to impress you that it's stifling all her natural reactions and affection. I'm not sure which yet. She has no reason to fear me—I'm her own choice; nor does she need to impress me, because she knows I'm not staying long. With those pressures off her, Penny is normal, affectionate, and *fun*. Only when you come into the picture does she regress.'

She told him of the much-loved straw hat, and how Penny hid it from him. He was baffled, and even more so when she continued, 'Penny panics if she spills tea or something on her clothes, and if she splits a seam it's the end of the world!'

'Sheena was always immaculate,' Rafe told her. 'Clothes were as important to her as men. She wouldn't let a grubby child anywhere near her. It was one of the things we quarrelled about. I suppose Penny is trying to be immaculate as well.'

'You said Sheena was hardly ever home,' Elisa reminded him, 'and why hasn't Janet done anything about it? Has she ever discussed it with you?'

'No. What are you getting at?'

Elisa sighed. 'I don't know. I wish I did.'

'Whatever Janet has or hasn't said, it was for Penny's sake. They're very close. Penny depends on her.'

'Penny's your daughter. Janet should be encouraging her to depend on you. It's curious, after losing her mother, that Penny shows no signs of missing Janet. It makes me wonder if they're really as close as you imagine.' Elisa picked up the poker and played with the fire, trying to think of the best way to phrase what she wanted to say next. Eventually she asked, 'Do you think it's possible *Janet* is the one who depends on *Penny*?'

'Why should she do that?'

Elisa put the poker down and turned to him. 'She might want to make herself indispensable by keeping Penny dependent on her, either to secure her job or because, well, maybe she's in love with you. She's—what—in her thirties? You're an attractive man and you have a lot to offer.'

'No,' he said positively, 'she knows her job's secure and there's never been anything personal between us. She doesn't feel that way about me.'

'A man is often the last to know,' Elisa told him hesitantly, thinking of her own suppressed feelings. 'It would also make it possible that she didn't fight against her illness out of loyalty to Penny, but because of fear of what you might find out when she was gone.'

'If you mean Janet has been *encouraging* Penny's trauma for her own ends—my God, that's Machiavellian!'

'I feel pretty Machiavellian even suggesting it,' Elisa admitted ruefully, 'especially as I might be barking up the wrong tree altogether. I'm only going on the things I know. If Penny rarely saw her mother, making Janet the mother substitute, then all her love and trust should be in Janet. There shouldn't be any trauma, certainly not a continuing one, because Janet has no need to teach Penny to fear you—but you said Penny's getting worse, not better. What do you make of it? I'm only certain that, with me, she is a happy laughing child and her anxiety only returns when you're around. So if you're not feeding that anxiety, who is?'

Rafe snapped upright in his chair. 'I'll soon find out. I'll fly to England and force Janet to tell me what the hell is going on.'

'Hey!' Elisa was so anxious to calm him down, she put a hand on his knee without realising it. 'Janet's still in hospital. That's not the time for a showdown, and the best thing you can do is stick close to Penny. If Janet has some kind of hold over Penny, now's the time to break and take advantage of it. Spend as much time as you can with her, be affectionate, loving, let her know how much you care for her.'

'Just how do you suggest I do that when she regards me as some kind of bogeyman?' he asked bitterly.

'Somebody's taught her that attitude. Only you can teach her differently. You'll think of something.' Elisa suddenly realised her hand was on his knee. She was about to withdraw it when he covered it with his own. Her heart stopped, then began beating so erratically that she could scarcely breathe.

'Penny's found a good friend in you. I'm grateful.' He leaned forward and kissed her on the cheek. It was the lightest, briefest of touches, and the marvel was it neither embarrassed nor stimulated her. The kiss had nothing to do with passion or provocation. It was more a gesture of understanding, his way of telling her that, after all the hiccups for their relationship, they were friends, too.

It was yet another tentacle reaching out to bind her to him but, for the moment, she didn't mind that, either. She felt warm and safe and comfortable—companionable feelings she would never in her wildest dreams have associated with Rafe Sinclair.

He must have been feeling the same way about her, because he didn't retreat into his study. He sat on with her in the room lit only by the intimate glow of the fire. Neither of them bothered to switch on a lamp or even thought of it. One hour slipped into another as they talked. He asked about her family and she told him her parents were teachers, her two younger sisters were both married with children, and the entire family lived in Berkshire or neighbouring Surrey.

'We're almost neighbours,' Rafe said. 'I live at Virginia Water.'

'Gosh, my youngest sister lives just up the road at Egham. I visit her a lot. I have a lot of friends there, too. Funny we should have to come all the way to Corfu to meet.' As soon as she said it, Elisa wished she hadn't. She'd made it seem as though their meeting was something special.

'Yes, funny,' he agreed, but Elisa's awkwardness vanished when he told her his only close relative was his father, who had retired to a cottage in Sussex. 'He spends some of the winter here. He says he likes the island when it's "sleeping", as it was when he built this house.'

'It's a pity you haven't got a large family like mine. What with sisters, nieces, nephews, aunts, uncles, cousins and heaven knows who else, Penny wouldn't have had time to become——' She broke off.

'Neurotic,' he supplied. 'I can believe it. You sound a close family. How come you haven't married?'

She was so lulled by the darkness, the quiet and the companionship, she almost told him the truth. She opened her mouth to do so, changed her mind and said fliply, 'Me? Oh, I haven't met the right millionaire yet. Well, tomorrow's Saturday and you're not working. Perhaps we'd better sort out what we're going to do over the weekend.'

He noticed both her hesitancy and her sudden change of subject. 'So you have your secrets, too, Elisa. I wonder what they are?'

She was doubly grateful for the darkness then, because it hid her painful rush of colour. To her relief, having put her on the hook, he took her off it by continuing, 'The weekend...what do you suggest?'

Perhaps he thought this companionship they'd established was close enough, and there were some avenues it was wise not to explore. He was right, of course, and together they worked out a plan of activities for the weekend that was best from Penny's point of view.

'Unless, of course, you want Sunday off?' asked Rafe, as an afterthought. 'You've been home every evening, and I had you down as somebody who likes the high life.'

'I can take it or leave it.' Elisa sensed dissension creeping in, stemming from his preconceived notion of her, however much he talked of wrong impressions and fresh starts. She didn't need a brain like Einstein to work out that he thought she was flighty.

'You must miss your friends.' He made it a statement not a question, and the plural was his idea of tact. He meant *friend*—Rich.

Elisa wasn't going to rise to the bait, and two could play the plural game. 'Penny and I often stop off for an ice-cream or drink when we're to-ing or fro-ing from some other resort. We see them often.'

'They must be surprised you're still around.'

'They were,' Elisa corrected. 'The general consensus is that I've landed myself a jammy job. No slavery, and the chance to explore the island, all expenses paid.'

'And what do you think?' Rafe asked.

'I think you'd better come out with whatever's on your mind.'

There was a pause, then he said, 'All right. I'd like to be certain you're not fooling around on the beach while Penny's left to her own devices.'

Elisa was quietly, deeply angry. 'You mean with Rich. I've explained about him, and I refuse to go on justifying myself. You shouldn't have forced me here in the first place if you thought I was irresponsible. I am at least consistent, which is more than you are. Not so long ago you were thanking me for being a good friend to Penny. I wish you'd make up your mind.'

By the time she'd finished speaking, her anger was tinged with hurt. Perhaps he was sensitive enough to pick it up, because he said, 'It looks as though I owe you another apology.'

'Don't do me any favours. Just stop getting at me unless I give you cause.'

'Fair enough.' He stood up suddenly and switched on a side lamp. The interlude was over. He was restless again, full of nervous energy. She'd had him all to herself, and mostly peacefully, for two hours. Now she'd lost him to whatever devil it was that was driving him. She wasn't at all surprised when he continued, 'I've got some work to clear up before the weekend.'

He was almost at the study door when she said, 'Rafe?'

'Yes?'

He turned and looked at her, and now the companionship was gone she was once more painfully aware of his animal magnetism. She wanted to keep him with her but, at the same time, she wished she'd let him go. 'Nothing,' she went on. 'It doesn't matter.'

Rafe came back and sat on the arm of the fireside chair, looking down at her. 'If something's on your mind, it matters. What is it?'

'You don't think much of summer workers, do you?'

'As a general rule, no.'

'Why?' she asked.

'They seem a pretty feckless, immoral bunch.'

Which explains your attitude to me, she thought, wondering if she was beating her head against a brick wall for nothing. But she had to try to break down his prejudice. 'That's a dangerous generalisation, as generalisations usually are. If you really want to know about summer workers, you should talk to Rich. He's a sociologist. He's doing a postgraduate thesis on them. That's why he's working at the café, so he can identify.'

'You mean there's a brain in with all that brawn somewhere? You surprise me, but it explains the attraction. Is he a millionaire as well?'

'A millionaire?' Elisa had forgotten her earlier flip remark. 'No, why?'

'Because you'd have it made, wouldn't you?' replied Rafe, and went away and left her.

He sounded, even to Elisa's disbelieving ears, like a jealous man. She sat on by the fire, staring at the study door firmly closed against her, wondering if at last she'd discovered exactly which devil it was that drove Rafe Sinclair to be so cruel and hurtful to her.

CHAPTER EIGHT

SATURDAY got off to a rocky start. Elisa, cooking breakfast, and Rafe, re-reading an old newspaper at the table, were painfully polite to each other, not having overcome the atmosphere they'd parted under the previous evening. They needed their little chaperon to turn the kitchen into a safe and domesticated place.

When Penny did come in, though, she only deepened the gloom. She was wearing one of her prim frocks, white socks and shiny black shoes. For all the world, thought Elisa with exasperation, as though the past four days hadn't happened and Janet Tilson still reigned supreme.

Rafe shot a baffled look at Elisa, and she responded swiftly by saying to Penny, 'It's a shorts and sandals day. The weather's great and we're going to the beach. I told you so last night, remember?'

'I always wear a frock when I go out with Daddy,' Penny replied, sitting sedately at the table.

'I can't think why,' Rafe remarked, unwinding his long frame from his chair and standing up so she could see he was wearing khaki shorts with his epauletted khaki shirt. He nodded to Elisa, who was wearing a similar outfit in denim, and added, 'Wouldn't you be more comfortable dressed like us?'

But Penny only looked so confused and anxious that he sat down again, saying wearily, 'Never mind. If you're happy as you are, that's all that matters.'

Elisa turned back to the cooker, as baffled as he was. To think this was the day when she'd hoped to show

Rafe how much Penny had improved! The smell of burning recalled her to what she was supposed to be doing, and she found she'd let her attention wander for too long. The bacon was grilled to a crisp, the toast was singed and she'd forgotten to poach the eggs.

Deeply conscious of the depressed silence behind her, she said as cheerfully as she could, 'It's a good job this is Corfu and there's no train to catch. Breakfast will be slightly delayed. I've forgotten to cook the eggs.'

Neither of them answered, and matters didn't improve when she put three plates of half-set eggs, dried-out bacon and curling toast on the table. She studied their expressions as they looked down at the unappetising mess, and didn't bother to sit down herself.

Suddenly she felt as though the long shadow cast by Janet Tilson—or perhaps it was Sheena—had reached out to subdue her as well as the Sinclairs. She wasn't going to let that happen. She refused utterly to behave like anybody but herself, and Elisa Marshall would never let a day die on her, no matter how grotty its beginning.

She put her hands under their chins, tipped their faces up to hers and grinned at them. 'Who says we declare a disaster and go out for breakfast?'

She couldn't have surprised them more if she'd suggested a walk on the moon, but then Rafe got to his feet and said, 'I'm with you,' and Penny breathed a hasty, 'Me, too,' as she pushed her plate away.

'Right,' Elisa declared, beginning to stack the plates. 'Today irresponsibility rules, OK? We'll be wickedly wasteful and have a lot of fun. Rafe, you bring the car round. Penny, pack your beachbag. The sooner we get going, the sooner we eat. I'm starving, so scoot!'

Penny fled, giggling, but Rafe lingered to help her clear the table, something he'd never done before. He looked devastatingly masculine with his bare arms and legs, but she wasn't going to let her soaring spirits be short-circuited by any more high voltage emotion.

When he told her, 'You've got a dotty streak,' she smiled.

Then she replied, 'I hope you have, too. Remember me telling you about the straw hat Penny hides from you? I want you to buy one for yourself and vandalise it so it looks like mine. It might help her sort out her attitudes if you demonstrated to her what you think is, or isn't, important.'

'I've got an old hat,' he replied thoughtfully. 'It's probably at the bottom of a wardrobe somewhere. I haven't worn it for years.'

Not since Sheena, she guessed, and wondered if he needed as much therapy as his daughter. She kept her thoughts to herself and responded lightly, 'Great. Go and find it. I'll soon finish up here. Don't say anything, just wear it. It's impressions we're after, not pep talks. Penny only gets nervous if she thinks she's being questioned.'

Rafe turned towards her from the cupboard where he'd just put the condiments away. 'Will you be satisfied when you've got us both in funny hats?'

'Not funny, uninhibited,' she corrected with a chuckle. 'And, no, I won't be satisfied, but it'll be a start. You Sinclairs are too serious by half.'

'You think life's a joke?'

'I don't let it get me down.'

'No, you don't—witness breakfast.' He studied her for a long moment, then reached out and tweaked her plait. 'You're good for us, Elisa,' he said, and walked out of the kitchen.

Elisa's spirits soared skywards. He'd said 'us', including himself with Penny, and although pulling her plait was no big deal it showed that he, too, was capable of shedding the restraint that characterised both of them. The day was improving rapidly, and she soon found out there was better to come.

When she left the kitchen and went into the hall to chase up Penny, the little girl was already coming down the last of the stairs. To her delight, she'd changed into shorts and a blouse. Only her hat was missing to show this day was different, but Elisa made no mention of that, she just exclaimed, 'I'm so pleased you've decided to dress the same as us. Daddy will be, too.'

'I've put my frock in my beachbag, just in case.'

Elisa was dying to ask, 'In case of what?' but she resisted the impulse, fearful questioning would drive Penny back into her shell. She slapped her own hat on her head and picked up her beachbag, already packed and waiting in the hall. She heard the Land Rover's engine, then the bleep of the horn. 'Come on,' she said, 'the last one out has to run round the car three times before getting in.'

They charged for the front door and fell out of it in a laughing jumble of arms, legs and beachbags, Penny slightly in front. 'I won,' she crowed.

'You won and I run,' Elisa groaned, dropping her beachbag and charging three times around the car, with Penny laughing in a way that made the effort worth while.

Rafe climbed out of the driving seat and asked, 'What's going on?'

Excitedly Penny started to explain, then stopped dead, her eyes rounding with awe when she saw the battered straw hat on her father's head. She never finished her explaining, just said, 'I won't be a minute,' and dashed back into the house.

Elisa, leaning against the Land Rover while her breath evened out, murmured, 'I think she's gone for her hat. That'll be another milestone passed, though we might never know exactly what her hang-up about wearing it in front of you was.'

'I think she'll start to talk when she stops worrying less. Either way, I'm not so bothered now I know she can still laugh. All thanks to you, and I know why. You're not so much dotty as just an overgrown kid.'

Was that a caressing note in his voice? It certainly wasn't critical, and she felt sufficiently light-hearted to tip his hat over his eyes and prompt, 'You know what they say—if you can't lick us, join us.'

'I'll bear it in mind.' The sound of the front door slamming made him turn from her. Penny was coming towards them, wearing her hat. Perhaps he noticed, as Elisa did, her self-conscious air, because he swooped her up, kissed her cheek and sat her in the back seat. 'Terrific,' he said. 'Now we all match.'

Penny's eyes glowed and Elisa's throat constricted. It was the first time she'd seen Rafe dare to behave like an affectionate father, but she didn't have time to get sentimental about it because next he swooped her up and dumped her in the front passenger seat. He was a different man from the surly brute who had first made such an ineradicable impression on her.

Human, she thought, and loving, although heaven only knew for how long. Not that she was bothered about that when he strapped himself in beside her and asked, 'Right, where does a bunch of hillbillies go on a day out?'

'Not hillbillies,' Elisa corrected him, 'just common or garden trippers.'

Rafe groaned.

'Don't be such a snob. What's wrong with that?'

He looked from her glowing face to Penny's and smiled. 'Nothing. Absolutely nothing at all.'

He drove them down to the coast road for breakfast. Penny chose what she called 'Rich's café' for breakfast. He wasn't on duty, but Sue was and she made a fuss of them, rolling meaningful glances from Rafe to Elisa whenever she thought nobody else was watching. Elisa could cheerfully have murdered her. She didn't need Sue's clowning to make her conscious of how attractively male Rafe was.

Apart from that, she was glad they'd called in because Barbara, her friend working at the school in Athens, had written to her, care of the café. She put the letter in her bag to read later, wondering what on earth Babs had to say that made the letter so thick. Babs' usual idea of communication was a brief postcard or a quick phone call.

When they'd eaten a full and leisurely English breakfast to make up for the one unceremoniously dumped into the bin at the villa, Rafe drove them north to Sidori, a sleepy fishing village where they swam, lazed and played.

By late afternoon Elisa was wondering if she was the only one who was conscious of there being a touch of magic about the day, marking it out as one to be remembered long after others had been forgotten. Since that early rocky start, everything had gone so wonderfully well.

Penny had overcome her self-imposed awe of her father, behaving as naturally as she did with Elisa. At the moment she was a little farther along the the beach, carrying water in her red plastic bucket to the moat around a lopsided castle she had built with friends she had made.

For a long while Rafe had sat and watched her, bemused, trying to equate the happily absorbed and carefree child with the self-effacing little shadow he had retrieved after Sheena's death. Now, however, he was laying back on the sand, his hat over his face, so relaxed himself that Elisa thought he was asleep.

She was lying next to him, face down on her towel, her face turned instinctively to his, her sleepy eyes opening every so often of their own volition, as though it was very important to check he was still there. Some time ago she'd loosened her hair to dry it after a cooling swim, and she'd been too lazy to do anything about it since, except to push it back when it fell across her face.

She remembered the day she'd first seen Rafe, when he'd got such a bad impression of her because she'd been fighting off Rich's playful attempts to bite her. Had it been Rafe she'd been wrestling with, he'd have gained an even worse impression, she thought, because she wouldn't have fought for long. He'd have had his bite— but it was his kiss that was really on her mind.

That searing, scorching kiss on another day, another beach, cynically demanding a response she'd been unable to deny. A heady, hateful kiss exchanged for all the wrong reasons, but unforgettable, if only because it posed the tantalising question of how she would react if his reasons were right.

She stirred, both contented and discontented to have him lying so relaxed beside her. He was such an unpredictable man that he was making her unpredictable, too. She'd wanted him to have a happy and satisfying day, and now she'd succeeded so well, she was vaguely irritated. If she wasn't careful, she'd be the one in need of therapy.

He'd been so charming, so considerate to her all day long, treating her like a favoured companion rather than a nanny whom circumstances had forced upon him. Her caveman had turned into a courtier, and still she wasn't satisfied. Even proof of her beneficial effect on Penny wasn't sufficient reward for her. Was she the sort of woman who, when given the moon, only cried for the stars?

I don't like myself, she thought. I did before I met Rafe, but not any more. I might have felt miserable when I walked away from Austyn, but I felt noble with it. I'd done the right thing. I could live with myself, even cry for myself a little and feel justified about that, too.

With Rafe it was so different. He didn't make her feel noble at all. He made her want to fight, scratch, kick, take on past ghosts or future threats—anything that stood between them, or stood between his seeing and wanting her as a desirable woman.

Which, considering she was employed in a position of trust in his household, was pretty rotten. She didn't like to feel rotten. Not only did she dislike herself, she didn't even know herself. This couldn't be her, Elisa Marshall, simmering like a repressed volcano behind a smiling face. This was some other woman Rafe Sinclair had created when he'd first looked at her with such scorn.

He made Austyn, who had once seemed such a threat to all she genuinely believed in, seem as safe as a teddy bear in comparison. With Austyn she'd been able to defend her principles. With Rafe, she didn't seem to have any at all.

And I do, she protested vehemently to herself. All this is an illusion, the effect Rafe has on me because he can be so damned primitive himself. Really, I'm a nice, civilised, social creature. I care what others think of me and what I think of myself. I'm not a primitive, grabbing what I want when I want it. I *hate* people like that. I don't want to become one, even for a little while. Or do I?

Elisa sighed, but not for the world could she have said exactly what she was sighing about. I hate you, Rafe Sinclair, she thought, but she could just have easily breathed, I love you...

Rafe moved, propping himself up on his elbow, proving he was no more asleep than she was. That was good for her ego but bad for her peace of mind, making her more confused than ever. She was deeply conscious of his closeness as he looked down at her, and of the softness in his voice when he asked, 'What were you sighing for?'

'The stars, I think.' It wasn't such a silly answer. No more ambiguous than her feelings, anyway.

'With the sun blazing down?'

'Just shows you how hard I am to please.' She meant to be flippant, but somehow she just sounded wistful.

'Sad, Elisa?' he asked gently. Some sand had fallen from his arm on to her bare back, and he brushed it away. Her body welcomed his touch and dreaded it. She was concentrating so much on showing no reaction, she was taken by surprise by his next question. 'Is it something to do with me?'

She rolled over on her back and looked up at him, thinking, When in doubt, brazen it out. 'No, why should it be?'

'I've stolen a fortnight of your year of freedom. I thought you might be resenting it.'

Elisa relaxed. For a moment she'd thought he'd guessed what havoc he could wreak on her emotions when he wasn't even trying. 'Oh, that,' she replied, relief making her reveal more than she'd intended, 'I'm coming round to thinking freedom's an illusion. Wherever we run, we're still trapped inside ourselves.'

'I didn't know you were running.' The arrested expression in his so-blue eyes made her realise how unguarded she'd been, and predictably he asked, 'What from?'

Annoyed with herself, she snapped, 'You sound like Rich and his wretched thesis. I was sick to death of that.'

'I'm sorry.' He sat up abruptly, as though she'd slapped his face, and stared out to sea.

She couldn't have hurt him, could she? Not Rafe! He was impervious to snubs. Yet he appeared hurt. The thought that he could be vulnerable troubled her so much, she sat up and touched his arm. 'I'm the one who should be sorry. Rich never believed my "year of freedom" story and kept on about it. It's his head I should have snapped off, but he's so darned nice I couldn't do it. I'm afraid I've made you a substitute target.'

'Because I'm not so nice!'

Elisa wished she could say something frivolous like 'Got it in one,' but she felt that this moment was too important to throw away, that if they didn't begin to understand each other now they would always be wrangling. She told him, 'My touchiness over my "year of freedom" story is my hang-up, nothing to do with you. I hate telling lies, but in this instance the truth isn't very pretty.'

She knew if he said something cutting, or even trite, she'd clam up and keep the truth to herself as she'd always intended. Rafe, though, said nothing, displaying a sensitivity she hadn't known he possessed. He was giving her the chance to continue or change the subject as she wished. In some strange way, that made her feel closer to him than during those wild moments a few days ago when she'd actually been in his arms.

And she told him the simple, unvarnished truth. 'I have a good friend at home, Lorna, who teaches maths. She has a husband, Austyn, who teaches physics. We'd known each other for years, but suddenly Austyn and I fell in love. Why it happened——' she shrugged her slender shoulders helplessly '—I don't know, but it did. We were all teaching at the same school, and Lorna was pregnant. An impossible situation, so I took off. There's nothing very glamorous about that, is there? Well, Austyn has a son now, so hopefully he's sorted himself out.'

'And you've sorted yourself out with Rich?'

Of all the questions she'd been expecting, that was the last one. She picked up a handful of sand and sifted it through her fingers, apparently absorbed in watching it fall back to the beach. After a moment she said quietly, 'I'm still not sorted out.'

'Then if Austyn was inevitable, Rich was a mistake,' Rafe replied just as quietly. 'Is that why you moved on, because you'd realised it?'

'Once you get an idea in your head, it's hard to shift,' Elisa told him. 'Rich and I were never lovers. I moved on because—because it was time.' Briskly she brushed the last particles of sand from her hand. She was drifting into dangerous territory and she didn't want to lie again. 'I think I'll go and help Penny with her castle.'

This time his hand touched her arm, restraining her, but gently. 'You don't have to run away from me, Elisa. I've made enough mistakes to understand a few, and I don't intend to make any more. That should make me a pretty safe place.'

She couldn't tell him how wrong he was nor, after that, make her escape—and the truth was that she didn't really want to. Even when they were fighting, she felt more alive with him than without. They lay down again side by side, talking of this and that and nothing in particular, but companionably so.

It dawned on Elisa, as one charmed hour merged with another, that to be completely content in the company of a man when nothing special was happening, or likely to happen, must be what real love was all about. She didn't let the thought frighten her. Rafe, too, must be content, or his restless streak would have shown and he would have been up and off somewhere in his abrupt way.

Her mind, tremulously at first and then with growing wonder, was beginning to explore the possibility that she and Rafe were finding their way towards something altogether more binding than understanding or even lust. She was beginning to hope so, in any case, because she really didn't know what else to do.

Her optimism seemed justified, for Rafe appeared every bit as reluctant to end the day as she was. When Penny's friends left the beach they built another castle for her, a far grander one—and so it should be, Elisa pointed out, since it was designed by an architect and decorated by an artist.

For some reason this gave Penny a fit of the giggles, and soon Elisa was giggling with her. They were happy and so everything was amusing but, after taking some

photographs, Rafe decided they were hysterical from
hunger and bundled them back into the Land Rover.

The sun was waning and they pulled on their sweaters,
then Rafe drove them south. Elisa brushed her hair and
began to plait it. Rafe reached across and stilled her busy
fingers. 'Don't do that,' he told her without taking his
eyes from the road. 'I like it loose.'

Elisa's hands dropped in her lap, a warm glow stealing
over her. That wasn't the sort of remark a man made
to his daughter's nanny. It denoted a special interest,
and a right to have a say in how she looked. Perhaps he
realised it, because his hand returned to the wheel and
his next remark was addressed to Penny. 'Don't fall
asleep before we've stopped for dinner.'

'I won't, Daddy. I'm much too hungry.'

They were driving through Corfu Town when he asked
them both, 'Anywhere special you'd like to eat?'

'Nowhere formal,' Elisa put in quickly, imagining the
sort of hotels or restaurants Rafe normally dined in,
'we're all wearing shorts. Kanoni's just south of here.
Why don't we take pot luck at a place we like the look
of?'

'It will be noisy and crowded. Kanoni's a trippers'
paradise.'

'It's also the most beautiful spot on the island, and
it's still light enough to see the bay. Besides, I thought
we were trippers ourselves today, and we've had a very
quiet time so far. It also has the advantage of being close,
and I'm hungry enough to eat a whole octopus.'

'Me, too,' Penny chipped in.

'Kanoni it is, then,' agreed Rafe amicably enough, and
within a few minutes he had parked and they were
walking along the front looking down at the beach with
a causeway linking it to a beautiful monastery, and

beyond, almost at the mouth of the bay, the enchanting tree-covered islet that helped to make the view so famous.

'That's Mouse Island,' Elisa told Penny, 'a bit of a special place for you.'

'Why?' Penny asked, staring at it.

'According to legend, it was once the ship taking Odysseus home after the Trojan War, but Poseidon, the god of the sea, got cross and turned it to stone. Odysseus's wife was Penelope—your namesake. Because he'd been away so long, she was being forced to marry again. She said she would when she'd finished weaving a tapestry. Every night she unpicked the work she'd done that day, and so remained a faithful wife.'

'I didn't know about the island, but Mummy told me the story of Penelope. She laughed, so I know it's funny.'

'Funny?' Puzzled, Elisa glanced at Rafe and saw that he, like the legendary ship, had turned to stone. It was only then she realised where her eagerness to whet Penny's appetite for Greek mythology had led her. It was a cruel jest that Sheena, a faithless wife, had named her daughter Penelope, but to laugh in the child's face was crueller still.

What Rafe must be thinking of her to rake this up she didn't dare imagine, but she sought desperately for some way to put it right. 'Funny?' she repeated. 'No, I don't think so. Mummy must have been laughing about something else. Adults sometimes do, you know. It's a beautiful story, and yours is a very special name.'

'Even if it's shortened to Penny? She never did that.'

'Specially if it's shortened to Penny,' Elisa told her, improvising wildly. 'That makes it friendly as well as special.'

To her relief Penny accepted that without quibble, and beamed, 'So I have a special name *and* a special island. Can we go out to visit it one day?'

'Sure.' She looked at Rafe. 'Tomorrow, on our way to your friends' barbecue?'

'That's fine by me,' he replied, and Penny's smile widened as she skipped on ahead.

'I'm sorry,' Elisa breathed to Rafe. 'I'll think before I open my big mouth in future.'

'Don't,' he replied surprisingly. 'You seem to be doing more good by rattling the skeletons in the family cupboard than I've ever done by hiding them.'

'You looked as if you'd like to murder me.'

'I frequently do, but I'm learning to reserve judgement,' he told her, and smiled in a way that put more of a caress than a sting in his words.

Elisa couldn't think of an answer, perhaps because her heart was thumping in the painful way that was becoming familiar whenever she thought that she and Rafe were sharing a special moment. Funny how a certain look or smile from him could mean so much more to her than an embrace from any other man.

Her thoughts flew to Austyn. Was she including him? She couldn't decide or even concentrate on him just then. The image of him she had carried for so long in her mind kept blurring and re-forming into Rafe's face, and that was as it should be. She was beginning to let go at last of an impossible love for one that, hour by hour, was becoming altogether more promising.

Her growing happiness would have made bread and cheese seem like the food of the gods, but they dined splendidly on shrimp soup, baked fish, green bean salad and cream-filled pastries. Penny drank the delicious local lemonade, and Rafe and Elisa a light white wine.

The restaurant was neither noisy or crowded, as Rafe had predicted, and they sat by a window overlooking the sea. Daylight faded and the lights came on, turning the coastline into a mysterious and magical place. They talked and talked, Penny contributing more than her share so that Rafe's eyes often settled on her in wonder. Then he would look at Elisa and her toes would curl in her sandals and she'd wish she'd had time to put on a touch of eyeshadow and a trace of lipstick.

They were treated as a family and it was easier to accept than object, and that gave her a lovely warm feeling. It seemed so *right*, so natural, the three of them dining together like this, the stormy incidents that had brought them together fading into no more than a half-forgotten memory. Like Austyn, she thought, but again he dropped out of her mind as though he no longer had a place there.

Again, like herself, she had a feeling Rafe didn't want the day to end. They lingered over their wine until Penny lost her vivacity and her eyes began to droop. 'Bedtime,' Elisa said, so regretfully that she felt selfish, but Penny only smiled sleepily and said she had room for another pastry.

'Not tonight,' Rafe told her firmly. He picked her up so naturally, and her head drooped on his shoulder so naturally, that it seemed incredible that only yesterday they had been treating each other with the polite formality of strangers.

Penny was asleep by the time they reached the car. They wrapped her in a travel rug and Rafe peeled off his jumper to put under her head as they settled her on the rear seat. A wind had got up and the night air struck chill after the heat of the day. Elisa shivered as she strapped herself into the passenger seat.

'Cold?' asked Rafe, looking at her as he switched on the engine.

'Only my legs. I'm better off than you are. I've still got my sweater on.'

'I'm all right.' He reached across and touched her thigh. Elisa froze for another reason, but he only said, 'Goose-pimples. The heater will soon cure those.'

She was so piqued that he could touch her without any apparent effect that she wondered whether, in gaining his companionship, she hadn't lost something else that was equally vital to their relationship—at least the one she envisaged. She needed reassurance, and as he drove south along the coast road she fished for compliments in a roundabout way by saying, 'It was a lovely day, wasn't it?'

'I'll never forget it.' Her hopes soared, then steadied as he added, 'It was the day I got my daughter back. You can't imagine what it meant, seeing her laugh, play with other children and, most of all, not stand on ceremony with me.'

Of course, Elisa thought, seeing his daughter behave like a normal child would be much more important to him than discovering he could get on well with his temporary employee. There was nothing wrong with his priorities—it was hers that were out of perspective. She felt rueful, but it served her right for being so selfish.

'All thanks to you,' Rafe went on, snatching a quick glance at her. 'You're a five-day wonder.'

That made her laugh. 'Thanks very much! A five-day wonder is over by the sixth day.'

'You know what I mean. You've been with us five days.' He snatched another glance at her. 'Still cold?'

'As warm as toast, thanks.' She looked over her shoulder at Penny, saw she was still fast asleep, and closed her own eyes. She only meant it to be for a moment, but she drifted off to sleep herself.

The journey home took little more than half an hour, and once, when he was driving through a resort where the nightlife was in full gear, Rafe had to stop because of a traffic hold-up. His eyes were drawn to Elisa, and he looked at her long and thoughtfully. There was enough light from a roadside taverna for him to see her face. It was turned towards him and, in sleep, it was as soft and defenceless as Penny's.

Rafe looked back at the road, but the traffic still wasn't moving. Irresistibly, his eyes returned to Elisa, dwelling on the curve of her cheek, the dark sweep of her eyelashes, the droop of her full lips. Immeasurably moved, he bent to kiss her silken hair.

It was the lightest of touches, but Elisa stirred, murmured his name and her hand came up to his cheek. He took it and kissed it and laid it gently back into her lap. She sighed and sank more deeply back into sleep. It was only then that he realised fully what he had done.

He'd been so pleased it was his name she'd breathed, but now he wished it had been somebody else's. Austyn's, Rich's, it didn't really matter, because it would have broken the spell she could weave about him even in her sleep.

His face was grim as he drove on. He thought he'd been prepared to pay any price for Penny being freed from her nameless and nebulous fears, but that hadn't included becoming entrapped himself—not by a girl who, for all her apparent guilelessness, rang the warning bell that Sheena had planted so deeply in his brain.

CHAPTER NINE

CAREFULLY as Rafe drove along the rutted track to the villa, not wanting to jolt his passengers too roughly from their sleep, there were some bumps he couldn't avoid. Elisa stirred without opening her eyes. She was trying to hold on to a dream, a very beautiful dream, in which Rafe had kissed her head and her hand as a lover might, making her feel treasured and desired.

Another bump, and wakefulness could no longer be denied. The dream receded but some of its magic remained, keeping her eyes closed and curving her lips into a smile. She was deeply conscious of Rafe beside her, the only part of reality she wanted to encourage.

The car stopped and the engine cut. She knew he was looking down at her and she lay passively, hoping the dream would repeat itself and the magic would last for ever. It was wishful thinking, of course. Rafe switched on the interior light and she had to open her eyes.

'Sorry to be such a sleepyhead,' she said, the huskiness of her voice having nothing to do with drowsiness. She couldn't quite define his expression, but she thought there was a certain tautness around his mouth, the mouth that had been so gentle and caressing in her dreams.

'I wonder if we'll ever stop saying sorry to each other?' he replied, as though the words had been forced from him. Elisa nearly choked. Not because of the roughness with which he spoke, but because she was reminded of a line from an old film: 'Love is never having to say you're sorry.'

Would they ever be like that, she and Rafe? She was in love with him, or something so very much like it that she could no longer tell the difference. She didn't even want to. She wasn't thinking of the future, as she had with Austyn. She was grasping every passing minute and trying to make a lifetime out of it. That was the effect Rafe had on her. Immediate. Urgent.

She sighed.

It was the softest of sounds, but it shattered the defences Rafe had been shoring up against her during the past half-hour of automatic driving and intensive thought. He knew it would be a colossal blunder to kiss her again, but the only thing that stopped him was Penny sitting up and asking dazedly, 'Where are we, Daddy?'

'Home.' Part of him was glad for the interruption, part was sorry. Now he'd never know whether Elisa wanted him to kiss her, was inviting him to. It was years since he'd been uncertain about a woman, and that was a challenge all by itself...

'Must I wake up or can I go back to sleep?' Penny asked.

The plaintive voice galvanised them both into action. They jumped out of the car, and, while Elisa unlocked the front door and went ahead switching on the lights, Rafe carried Penny up to her room. Her eyes were open, but her curly head rested against his shoulder and her little arms were round his neck.

It was confirmation that she'd become his own little girl again. Trusting, loving and unafraid. Rafe looked at the shapely, graceful figure of Elisa walking ahead of him, and wondered if gratitude for this little miracle was the real reason why he couldn't sustain any hostility towards her.

When he put Penny down in her bedroom, he knelt down and kissed her on the cheek. 'I'll give you a piggy-back ride up tomorrow if you're awake enough, just as I used to when you were tiny.'

Penny's sleepy eyes opened wider. 'I don't remember. Was that before you got cross with me and sent me away?'

Elisa was turning back the covers on the bed, but she looked round. Her eyes met Rafe's, then he ruffled Penny's hair and asked gently, 'Who put that nonsense into your head?'

'It's not nonsense, it's——' Penny stopped suddenly. Her head drooped. She leaned it against Rafe's shoulder and went on, 'I'm tired, Daddy. I want to go to bed.'

Elisa was afraid he would press more questions on her before she was ready to answer, and she leaned forward and gripped his other shoulder warningly.

He looked up at her, his eyes icy with anger. She frowned and shook her head, and, after a fraught moment when the issue hung in balance, he nodded. When he spoke again to Penny it was lightly, as though he'd forgotten the question he was burning to know the answer to. 'Of course you're tired, but before you go to sleep I want you to know I never got cross with you and sent you away. I wanted to keep you very much, but so did Mummy and she won. Now you're back with me for good, which was what I always wanted, so neither of us have got anything to worry about. All right?'

Penny's head nodded on his shoulder.

'Good,' Rafe told her. 'If you want to talk about it some more any time, just let me know, and I'll explain it all.' He lifted her face and kissed her cheek. 'Now, off to bed with you before you fall asleep on your feet.'

Penny hugged him without saying anything, then he stood up, ruffled her hair affectionately and left the room. It didn't take Elisa long to get her into bed. Penny was too tired to want a bedtime story, but Elisa sat by her bed until she was certain her sleep was sound.

Then she showered and changed into her jeans and black jumper, brushing her towel-dried hair and looking at her face thoughtfully in the mirror. After a while she discovered she'd been staring at herself without seeing anything, her mind hopping from the problem of Penny to the problem of Rafe, until they became inextricably mixed.

She sighed again, realised that was becoming a habit and pulled herself together. Her hand hovered over her make-up and fell to her side. She didn't want Rafe to think she was making herself especially attractive for him. After what Penny had said, he could do without that kind of distraction. More's the pity, her selfish side said, but that was understandable because she was aching to comfort him. Not that he was the sort of man who would appreciate comfort.

He was more likely to scorn it—and yet sometimes she sensed he was reaching out for her in a way that wasn't physical. Or was she getting dreams and wishful thinking mixed up with reality again, as she had when she'd woken in the car? She didn't know, but she had to make a conscious effort to smother another useless sigh.

When she went downstairs, there was no sign of Rafe. The beachbags were in the hall, so he'd unpacked the car. She carried them into the kitchen and sorted them out. She slung the peg-bag over her shoulder, picked up the towels and went out to the patio at the back. She didn't bother to switch on the patio lights, there was enough coming from the windows and the open door.

She shook the sand out of the first towel before hanging it up, and Rafe said, 'Thanks.'

Elisa spun round. He was sitting at a table just outside the stream of light, and he was brushing sand off himself. 'Sorry,' she said, 'I didn't know you were there.'

'That's all right. I like sand in my brandy.'

'I'll get you another,' she offered.

'I can get it.' The chair scraped as he stood up. 'You're not my nanny.'

He walked past her and into the house. She felt snubbed, and she didn't like it any more than he had earlier in the day. The trouble with wearing your heart on your sleeve, she thought, is that it gets knocked about a lot. But she wasn't sorry she'd disturbed him. Sitting out here brooding all by himself wasn't good for him. Then she wondered what made her think she knew best for him when she didn't even know what was best for herself.

There was another sigh to be smothered, then she pegged out the towels and went back into the kitchen. She made a fresh pot of coffee, and while it was perking she thrust the forgotten letter from Barbara into the back pocket of her jeans and started rinsing the salt and sand from the swimsuits.

A hand came over her shoulder and held a balloon glass with a generous measure of brandy in it in front of her eyes. Elisa froze. He had come up noiselessly, and he was so close she only had to lean back to be in his arms. 'Peace offering,' he said, his voice so close to her ear she could feel his breath, and something within her curled up with ecstasy. 'I did an Elisa—snapped the wrong head off. Sorry.'

That word again. Sorry. Love is . . . she recalled again, but then it all changed and became: Love is feeling like this just because he's being nice to me. There was a cloth on the draining-board. She wiped her hands without a word, took the glass and turned to him.

Rafe stepped back, but not very far, and raised his glass. 'Friends?' he asked, smiling at her.

'Friends.' If she was a little breathless, it was because he could be so charming, and his closeness was playing havoc with her senses, as usual. They both drank, watching each other. Elisa's eyes watered. She blinked rapidly and confessed, 'I'm not used to drinking straight spirits.'

'Don't expect me to put lemonade in it. I wouldn't even dream of doing that to ouzo.'

'You're not much good at humouring the peasants, are you? Would you shout at me if I said I liked it in coffee?'

'Anything to stop you pulling faces.' Rafe moved away, which saddened her heart but helped her breathing. She watching him pour her a coffee just as she liked it, black with one sugar. He must have been watching her more closely than she'd realised. As he added the brandy to the coffee, he went on, 'Stop fussing around that sink and come into the sitting-room. I've got a good fire going.'

Elisa turned hurriedly back to her rinsing. 'Be with you in a couple of secs.'

'Now,' he said, 'I want to talk to you. That can wait until morning.'

'I don't want to get up to a sinkful of washing.' She didn't know why she was being difficult. Perhaps because she automatically resisted anybody who bossed her about, and Rafe could be bossier than most. She turned the tap on full blast.

His hand came over her shoulder and switched off the tap, and this time his voice in her ear reminded her, 'I said *now*, Elisa.' He put his hands on her waist and lifted her aside as though she were a featherweight. He opened the kitchen door, threw the bowl out on to the patio and closed the door again.

'And you call me scatty!' she breathed.

'If you can throw my breakfast away, I don't see why I shouldn't do the same to your washing. Do I have your full attention now, Miss Marshall?'

Elisa didn't know whether she was being bullied, charmed or flirted with, but he was smiling at her and she couldn't help but smile back. 'Certainly, Mr Sinclair,' she mocked.

'About time,' he grumbled, but he was smiling. They picked up their drinks and as they walked through the hall to the sitting-room he put an arm companionably across her shoulders.

The goose-pimples she suffered from then were entirely pleasurable. She *liked* this relaxed and friendly man, which was something altogether different to being fascinated by him. She knew how unreliable his moods were, none better, yet she wanted to believe he'd always been like this before Sheena had soured him. If so, like his daughter, he was curable...

They sat opposite each other in armchairs pulled up towards the fire. It was a cheerful one, the coals glowing, the logs crackling with flames. She picked up a poker because she did love playing with a fire, but he took it from her. 'Don't start fussing again. The fire doesn't need it. I'm a better Boy Scout than you are.'

'Is that where you learned your novel way with laundry?'

He smiled and stretched back lazily in his chair, his long legs tangling with hers, which didn't seem to bother him, although she self-consciously moved hers away. Like herself, he had showered and changed into jeans and sweater. He'd switched on only two wall lights, and their effect was muted so that the fire was the principal source of light.

He looked so handsome, so masculine, so utterly at ease, that she was swamped with love for him. It had been bad enough at times on the beach, but here in the quiet room, within the intimate circle of the fire's glow, she was almost overwhelmed by the need to reach out and touch him. She sipped her coffee, hoping the brandy in it would lull her nerves.

He'd said he'd wanted to talk to her, but as he drank his brandy he didn't seem to be in a hurry to say anything. She began to wonder if it was her company he really wanted and her senses fluttered anew. She drained her cup and put it down on a side table.

'Another one?' he asked.

She shook her head, not trusting her voice.

'A sandwich?' he offered.

That was strange. He was treating her as a guest, somebody special enough to be pampered. She was the one who usually did the running around. She discovered she liked him pampering her, although she replied, 'No, thanks. I'm happy as I am.'

'Happy enough to stay with me?' he asked softly.

She wanted to put her hands over her heart to stop its sudden agonising thumping. She could scarcely believe her ears, and yet it would have been even more incredible if all this emotion she'd been bottling up was a one-way thing. No, today—with all its right bits and even the wrong—had worked its magic on him, too.

'S-stay?' she whispered, needing the right words from him to anchor the magic so it wouldn't drift away like another bittersweet dream.

'An extra week. A fortnight, if you can manage it. What Penny said this evening shows she's at a crucial point in her recovery. She very nearly came out with the whole story. I can't risk handing her over to another nanny who knows nothing about her. She needs you.' Rafe leaned forward and grasped her wrist. 'The same terms will apply, and I'll throw in a bonus.'

She stared down at his hand, glad of the fire's glow to hide the dull flush of humiliation that stained her cheeks. She felt numb. It was Penny who needed her, not him, and he'd made it plain enough he'd do whatever was necessary to get what Penny wanted.

Elisa knew he'd deliberately duped her. He'd charmed and cosseted her until she'd become putty in his hands. The worst part was that she couldn't loathe him, only herself for being such a love-struck fool.

She couldn't seem to take her eyes off his hand on her wrist. It was brown and strong and, rotten as he was, she wanted to bend her head and rub her cheek against it. She watched his hand move from her wrist, take her hand and hold it. 'Please, Elisa,' he said.

So he was ready to plead. She hated that. She'd rather have him bullying her than begging. He might kick her pride all over the place, but she didn't have it in her to do the same to his. She carefully removed her hand from his and, to play for time, she replied, 'You've certainly sprung this on me. Another week?'

'At least. I'll try to finish my work by then, but if you can manage a fortnight I can use that final week to gradually take over caring for her myself so the new routine is established before you leave. That will make it easier for Penny, and it will give me plenty of time to find a suitable permanent nanny. Sheena chose Janet, but I'll be looking for the right character and personality as well as qualifications.'

'Then you won't be having Janet back?'

Rafe's face grew grim. 'No. If it was Sheena who damaged Penny, Janet must have known. She could have shielded her, or at least told me about it. She did neither. And if it was Janet——' He broke off, and when he continued it was to say, 'I'll make a quick trip to England while you're here to see her and get things straight. I can be there and back within twenty-four hours.'

'What I don't understand,' Elisa said, frowning, 'is why she had to be away for six weeks. I didn't think of it at the time, but people needing appendectomies don't need all that time to recover.'

'There were complications, including a kidney infection, and she was generally in a low state of health. I thought she'd worn herself down worrying about Penny, so the least I could do was give her six weeks to rest and recover properly.' He leaned towards her again and Elisa moved back in her chair. She didn't want him touching her again. His reasons still weren't right.

'Well, Elisa?' he asked. 'Will you spare me that extra fortnight? You'll still have two for your island hopping.'

'I'm not the only one involved. There's Barbara.' Belatedly she remembered the letter in her back pocket and she pulled it out. 'I've been carrying this around all day and I still haven't opened it.'

'Read it now,' said Rafe, standing up and taking her cup from the side table. 'I'll make some more coffee.'

Elisa opened the envelope. There were several pages of Babs' hurried scrawl and, with Rafe so much on her mind, she found it hard to concentrate. She had to read it twice before she got the full gist of it. Babs had been so excited, it was full of exclamation marks, crossings out and underlining. She was staring into space when Rafe put a fresh cup of coffee beside her.

He sat down and studied her face. 'Bad news?'

'No—no, nothing like that. Just a bit of a bombshell.' Elisa picked up her coffee and the smell told her there was brandy in it before she sipped it. 'You don't have to get me drunk to make me agreeable. You can have your extra two weeks.'

He smiled and again she moved back as he leaned towards her and said, 'Thank you, Elisa. As I've said, I'll make it more than worth your while.'

'I'm already overpaid and don't thank me, thank Babs. She's no longer a problem, at least as far as you're concerned. With me, it's a different matter. The deputy head of the language school is an American, and she's flying to the States with him when the school breaks up in June to get married. She'll be honeymooning in——' Elisa referred to the letter '—in Wyoming until school re-starts in September, then she'll be living permanently in Athens.'

'So you've lost your travelling partner? What will you do?'

'Find another, or tour by myself. I'm not ready to go home yet.' She was glancing through the letter again and smiled. 'She says they mean to start a family pretty soon because she's turned thirty, poor old dear.'

'How old are you, Elisa?'

'Pushing twenty-six.'

'I was ten when you were born.'

Elisa was happy for Babs but twice as miserable for herself, and to cover it she lightly, 'Did you have a green velvet suit and clay pipe?'

'Pardon?'

'I thought once that you must have looked like Bubbles when you were a boy—you know, the Millais painting.'

Rafe laughed and, miserable as she was, she enjoyed watching and listening to him. She wasn't surprised when he told her, 'My hair was never that long, and I was never that angelic.'

'That I can believe.'

His eyebrows rose. 'Do I detect disapproval? I thought we were friends.'

She wanted to accuse him of buttering her up to make her stay longer. Afraid, though, of revealing the depth of her resentment, she changed the subject. 'Remember saying once you believed I reminded Penny of her mother? There's a photograph of Sheena in her room, and I'm nothing like her. We're both fair, but our faces are entirely different.'

Rafe nudged a log on the fire with his boot, sending a shower of sparks up the chimney. Then he replied curtly, 'You give the same impression. You have the same confidence, the same swinging walk, the same——'

'Hang on,' Elisa interrupted, irritated by the increasing contempt in his voice, 'I wasn't walking when you first saw me. I was lying on the beach.'

'I'd seen you a couple of times before that. You were walking along the beach road while I was driving through to town. The similarity was striking.'

Elisa had almost finished her coffee, and there'd been enough brandy in it to give her the courage to say, 'You disliked me on sight because of some cock-eyed notion that I was like the wife you loathed!'

'I've apologised for that.'

So he had, but it still stung. 'You were going to mention something else about us you thought was the same. What was it?'

'The same sexuality.'

'Oh.' Elisa hadn't been expecting that. She recovered enough to protest, 'Well, I don't chuck it about, do I?'

'It wouldn't matter if you did,' replied Rafe coldly. 'I'm cured of the obvious. I go for something a bit more subtle now.'

Damn it, he'd hurt her again. Really hurt her, too much to protest when he stood up and told her curtly, 'If you'll excuse me, I have some work to catch up on.'

He went out of the room, taking with him the magic from the day and the dream from her heart.

CHAPTER TEN

SUNDAY morning was remarkable for two things. Elisa cooked an excellent breakfast and Rafe behaved as though they'd never exchanged a cross word. Elisa, with deepening scepticism, thought he must be afraid she'd go back on her word and refuse to stay the extra fortnight—which showed how little he really knew her.

After breakfast they went for a walk through the olive groves, Rafe holding Penny's hand and Elisa bringing up the rear with her bag stuffed with art materials slung over her shoulder. When they came to an upthrust of rocks, she stayed to do some sketching, thinking that, the more she dropped out of the picture, the more Rafe and Penny would become used to each other's company.

She watched them until the path twisted and they were lost to view, then she climbed the rocks until they levelled out and the trees began again. From her vantage point she could look down over the groves to the sea. She settled down and began to draw quickly, thinking this would make a good watercolour if she ever found the time.

Perhaps during the long, cold winter in England, when there would be no sun to put warmth into the colours, no Rafe to put meaning into her life. She wished—oh, drat, she thought, I wish too many things that are never going to come true. The sketch was finished. She closed the book and brought out a smaller one she kept closed with an elastic band.

Elisa slipped the band over her wrist and looked through it page by page. This was her secret indulgence, for over these pages her love for Rafe spilled out, capturing him from every angle and in every mood. Well, almost. There wasn't one of him with lover's eyes. She'd tried many times to draw him with the soft glow of love muting the clarity of the blue, but none had worked out right. She would have to see it for herself to capture it.

Elisa heard them coming back before she saw them. They were laughing, so something was going right somewhere, and she hastily re-packed her bag and began the descent from the rocks. It was much harder, and seemed a lot farther, going down then coming up, so that she began to wonder if she had chosen the right place.

She was nearly down and scrabbling frantically for a foothold when she felt Rafe's hands on her waist. He lifted her down and smiled. 'I don't think you're ready for Everest yet.'

'Not in these shoes, at any rate.' They both looked at her open-toed sandals. She wondered why he was still holding her by the waist, and whether he guessed her breathlessness was not from climbing.

'We missed you,' he said, releasing her with every sign of reluctance.

'Yes,' Penny agreed, holding up a bunch of wild flowers. 'I had to pick these all by myself.'

'We wouldn't have left you at all if we'd known you were going to get stuck,' Rafe told her, taking Penny's hand as they began the long walk down to the villa.

'I wasn't stuck,' Elisa protested, falling in beside him, and making the mistake of looking at him. He was smiling down at her. Her heart somersaulted and she conceded, 'All right, I was.'

He was too close, which wasn't good for her, and she was just going to fall behind when his arm came across her shoulders in that companionable way he'd adopted yesterday. She knew now that it was a ploy, a way to draw her into the circle, make her feel wanted. She wasn't going to be duped into cloud cuckoo land again—and yet she stayed where she was. The needs of the flesh were cancelling out the urgent warnings of the brain.

Slowly, stupidly, but unavoidably, she began to feel happy.

Elisa was still wary enough not to expect another magical day, but there was no denying Rafe's charm and good humour put a certain sparkle into it. When they were back at the villa she asked him, 'How do we dress to visit your friends?'

'Frocks would be right, but nothing that a barbecue might spoil, and pack your swimsuits.'

Elisa didn't possess a frock. She teamed an Indian cotton skirt of deep blue and white with a white blouse that tied below her breasts to leave her tanned midriff bare. It was hot and getting hotter, so she tied her hair into a ponytail to keep it clear of her neck. For the first time since she'd met Rafe she wore make-up, pink lipstick and a touch of deep blue eyeshadow.

She couldn't have looked at her reflection more nervously if this had been a date her whole future depended on. No, she was definitely not overdone—under, if anything—but she was still more 'dressed up' than he'd ever seen her. A touch of perfume, her feet slipped into her best sandals with little heels, and she was ready.

Penny, dressed in a pink and white frock with her fair curls gleaming, didn't notice any difference, but she flattered herself that Rafe did. He was wearing lightweight fawn trousers with a matching shirt and a dark brown tie, and she found herself thinking wistfully, If only he were mine... He crooked an arm for both of them and said, 'Two pretty ladies. I'm honoured.'

Penny reached up for one arm, Elisa slipped hers through the other and he added appreciatively, 'Mm, you smell nice, too.'

As he led them out of the front door Elisa leaned forward to look at Penny and said, 'I think we're supposed to say "Thank you, kind sir".' They said it in unison, then they were climbing into the Land Rover. Rafe put the beach-bags in the back and Elisa raised her eyebrows when she saw his briefcase among them.

'A touch of business in with the pleasure,' he explained as he got in beside her.

They lunched at Benitses, took a boat over to Mouse Island, and then Rafe looked at his watch and said it was time they were on their way to the Carstairs' villa. 'You'll like Anne,' he told her as they joined the town-bound traffic. 'She's nearly sixty, but you'd never guess it. Her husband Tony's a stockbroker. He won't be joining her until the end of June, but she has a couple of grandchildren, Nikos and Markos with her, both older than Penny. There'll be plenty of other children there, though. The villa is usually like a mini United Nations. Anne has the knack of making all nationalities feel at home.'

'You sound as though you've known her a long time,' Elisa observed.

'Since I was born. The Carstairs have had a villa here as long as my family.'

The traffic thinned out at the other side of town, and apart from an occasional car or delivery truck they had the road to themselves. Rafe had fallen silent, as though he had something on his mind, and Elisa and Penny shared comments on the beautiful views.

'Here we are,' Penny told Elisa as Rafe spun the wheel and they went down a dirt track at considerably reduced speed. 'I've been here before.'

'Lucky you,' Elisa breathed. Rafe was parking next to a group of cars, and she was looking up at a lovely white-painted villa with verandas on both storeys over-looking the sea and a deep, wide patio in front which was thronged with brightly dressed people.

There were curving approach steps on either side. Rafe took his briefcase from the back and led them up the nearest flight. 'We'll leave the beach-bags where they are until we want them,' he told Elisa, and nodded down towards the beach. 'There are changing cabins down there, so if you and Penny want a dip before I'm ready, just go ahead.'

He steered them through the crowd on the patio. It took a lot of time. He knew everybody and soon Elisa's head was reeling with all the introductions. It would take her a month of applied effort, she thought, to sort out who everybody was.

They made an equally slow progress through the house. Maids were circulating with trays of drink and food. By this time she'd registered that the Carstairs lived extremely well. Her Indian cotton looked very homespun among all the silks, and thank God she hadn't worn her frayed cut-offs!

Still Rafe pressed on, until they were on another patio at the back of the house, surrounded by flowerbeds and a heavily wooded garden. The crowd was much thinner here, the noise of chatter mercifully less, and then a rather buxom woman with red-tinted hair and a green silk afternoon frock that smacked of Bond Street came towards them with arms outstretched.

'Rafe!' They embraced each other and he kissed her cheek, then she bent to kiss Penny's cheek. Very politely, Penny greeted her and kissed her in return.

'Anne,' said Rafe, 'this is Elisa.'

Anne looked at her searchingly, and not altogether approvingly, Elisa thought, but then the carefully made-up and slightly bulbous hazel eyes became veiled and she couldn't have been more courteous as she made her welcome. 'Penny's new nanny,' she said. 'It's so nice to meet you at last. Rafe's told me so much about you.'

Had he, indeed? They must keep in very close contact. And what did she mean about 'at last'? Elisa counted up and found it was only six days since she'd started working for Rafe. Anne seemed to be showing an extraordinary amount of interest in a common or garden nanny.

This suspicion deepened when Anne took her by the arm, Penny by the hand, and led them to a table. 'Come and sit down and get your breath back after fighting your way through that crowd.' She looked over her shoulder and added, 'Rafe, will you join us?'

'Be right there,' he replied, and went back into the house.

Anne chatted lightly and so charmingly that Elisa wondered why she was on her guard, and yet she was. She was glad when Rafe returned with three drinks on a tray. 'Beer for me,' he said as he unloaded it, 'lemonade for Penny, and ouzo and lemonade for you, Elisa.' He sat down, smiled at her and added softly, 'Peasant.'

Elisa smiled back and then, aware of Anne's eyes going from his face to hers and back again, explained, 'Rafe's trying to cure me of adulterating my ouzo with lemonade. It's one of my tripper's habits he finds very hard to live with.'

Did that sound too intimate? Anne's eyes had become veiled again, but Elisa thought, Drat, I can't watch every word I say, and why should I when our association is entirely innocent?

There was a sound of laughter, followed by childish shouts from among the trees up the hilly garden. 'Nikos, Markos and the others are playing hide and seek,' Anne explained.

Penny jumped off her chair, her face eager. 'Can I play, too?' she asked.

'Sure,' Elisa and Rafe said together, and Elisa added, 'Do you want me to come with you?'

'No, I know Nikos and Markos.' Then she was running across the patio and up the slope towards the noise.

'Good heavens, what a difference!' Anne exclaimed. 'She wouldn't leave Janet's side last time you brought her here.'

'She's under new management, and blossoming,' Rafe replied. 'She's my daughter again. I have Elisa to thank for that.'

Anne covered his hand with hers. 'I'm so pleased. I knew it could only be a matter of time, although I didn't think it would be this quick. She seemed pretty traumatised to me.'

'Without Janet, Penny's a different child. It's as though a cloud's been lifted from her or, more accurately, Elisa's blown it away. Elisa doesn't stand on ceremony with her, and it works. Penny responds.'

Anne looked at Elisa without a trace of her former hostility. She even sounded different as she said, 'Well done, Elisa. Rafe said he needed a miracle. I'm glad he's found one.'

Elisa was about to stammer that she was no such thing, when a soft but distinctive voice said, 'Rafe.'

If it was a summons, Rafe responded swiftly to it. He got to his feet and smiled at a slender woman who stood, not by the open patio doors, but by another farther along. She was delicately lovely, with black-lashed grey eyes and titian hair curling over her head, stray wisps and tendrils touching her forehead and ears. She wore a frock of ivory satin that was so simple, so beautifully cut, it must have cost a fortune.

'Angélique,' Rafe said, and something within Elisa died.

She watched him walk towards the elegant vision, kiss her cheek and slip an arm around her waist to lead her back into that private room. She had to mock the pain she felt to make it bearable, and tell herself that now she knew how Cinderella felt when her coach turned back into a pumpkin—robbed.

Elisa wished that whatever was dying within her would get it over and done with. She rather thought it must be hope, because now she could see there never *had* been any hope for her and Rafe. For him, physical attraction was as far as it went, and Angélique was the reason he could master it so much better than she could. What a fool she'd been to overlook anything as obvious as another woman. A man like Rafe was hardly likely to be without one, now was he?

'Who is Angélique?' Elisa asked, finding it painful just to say the name.

'My daughter. She married young and was widowed by the time she was twenty-two. It was very tragic. Dimitri was a Greek hotelier. He died of a pulmonary embolism following a minor operation. The twins, Nikos and Markos, were born six months later, so he never saw them.'

Elisa expressed her sympathy and Anne smiled. 'It happened nine years ago. Angélique had the twins to live for and everybody was very supportive—particularly Rafe, but of course they'd known each other all their lives. The mystery was why *they* didn't marry. Everything pointed that way, but then——'

Anne broke off and Elisa, wondering where all this was leading, guessed, 'Angélique met Dimitri?'

'Yes, and Rafe was very wild in those days. He didn't steady up until he took over the family business. It was failing, you know. He's done a marvellous recovery job in spite of——'

'Marrying Sheena?' prompted Elisa, knowing she was being nosy, but wanting to learn all she could about Rafe.

'Precisely. What do you know about her?'

'Virtually nothing.'

There was a rush of movement and three children came running towards them, followed by a dark-haired young woman. 'Ah, my grandchildren, Nikos and Markos,' Anne introduced, 'and Gwen, Angélique's au pair.'

The third child was Penny, and she bobbed around impatiently while the introductions were made, then said to Elisa, 'Is it all right if I go swimming?'

'Of course. I'll come with you.' But Anne put a restraining hand on her arm.

'Gwen will look after them. You can join them after we've had our little talk.'

The children were off, closely followed by Gwen, and Elisa was left with an impression of merry-faced identical twins with large brown eyes and unruly mops of curly red-brown hair.

'Now, where was I?' Anne murmured, and it was then Elisa realised her hostess was as keen to tell her about Rafe and Angélique as she was to find out. 'Ah, yes— Sheena. She came into our lives seven years ago. The twins were eighteen months old, Angélique had been widowed for two years, and the pressures of business had steadied Rafe and made him responsible in a way that was remarkable. They'd always been close, and it seemed to me that summer they were growing closer— then he met Sheena.'

Elisa looked down at her drink and swirled the glass so that the ice-cubes clinked. 'I can't believe Sheena was lovelier than Angélique,' she told Anne, because that was the uppermost thought on her mind.

'She wasn't. What Sheena had was something different entirely. There was something about her—a way of walking, a way of holding her head—that challenged every man in sight, and Rafe is very much a man.' Anne leaned back in her chair and surveyed Elisa humorously. 'I was prepared to hate you on sight because you have the same quality.'

So that was what the hostility was all about. Elisa had suffered the same from Rafe, and she was tired of it. 'I'm not Sheena,' she said with an edge on her voice, 'and if I offer a challenge it's a passive one. I don't make a habit of following it up.'

Anne patted her arm again. 'I realised that quickly enough, or Rafe would never have employed you. One bad experience with a girl like Sheena is enough to cure any man for life.'

'Well, if she couldn't be happy with Rafe, I shouldn't think she could be happy with anyone,' Elisa said, and then wondered if she'd said too much.

But Anne only agreed. 'That was the problem. Sheena had to keep proving she was irresistible. It was an ego thing. She was, quite simply, incapable of being faithful, and Rafe was incapable of being the cuckolded husband. He turned her out. It was so inconceivable to her that any man would want to be rid of her that she turned nasty and struck back through Penny. The rest, I suppose, you know.'

Elisa nodded, but she'd had too much boxing in the dark with Rafe to tolerate any more, and she asked, 'Why are you telling me all this?'

'I'm sure Rafe hasn't, and it's something you should know. He hides his wounds just as Angélique does. They have another opportunity now to discover how deep their feelings are for each other, and it would be a great pity if anything interfered with that.'

'In fact, you're warning me off.'

'What a very frank young lady you are. I can appreciate that. Can you appreciate that after all they've been through they deserve their chance?'

'Yes,' Elisa agreed, because she had no choice. 'Frankly, though, if Rafe and Angélique are in love, there's nothing I or anybody else could do about it—and I deeply resent the inference that I'm like Sheena and set my cap at a man just for kicks.'

'Now I've upset you. I'm sorry, my dear, I can only plead that old as I am, and grown up as Angélique is, I'm still her mother. I only have to see one of my chicks threatened and up come my feathers and I'm cackling out a lot of nonsense.' Anne smiled in a way that made herself—and Elisa's anger—seem ridiculous. 'Am I forgiven?'

She held out her hand and Elisa couldn't help but take it. 'Forgiven,' she said, 'but don't you think it's a good idea to bury the past and let the future take care of itself?'

Anne pulled a face. 'I'm not a great lover of platitudes.'

'Neither am I,' Elisa admitted, and they both laughed. 'I think I'd better go down to the beach to give Gwen a hand.' She tried not to look at the door to that private room, just as she tried to tell herself it was no business of hers if Rafe and Angélique didn't want to join the other guests. 'If Rafe wonders where Penny is, will you tell him?'

'Certainly, although it might be a while before he comes looking. He'll be showing Angélique the designs he's made for her new villa. She's selling the one she has on the Kanoni peninsula and building here. I expect they'll also be discussing the holiday complex Rafe's designing for the Kapsoskis brothers. She married the eldest of them, Dimitri. She's a trustee for the twins' share in the business, and she takes an active part in running it.'

'I see,' Elisa replied, and she did. Not only was Angélique lovely, and quite apart from the fact that her sons needed a father and Penny needed a mother, there were excellent business reasons for Rafe marrying her. Where did that leave herself? On the outside, where she'd always been.

She tried to forget her troubles on the beach. It wasn't easy, because there was so little for her to do. Penny was playing happily with the other children, which was as it should be. Eventually everybody from the villa trooped down to the beach and the barbecue was lit.

Elisa, without the least bit wanting to, gathered a group of eligible—and not so eligible—men around her. If Rafe noticed, he gave no sign. It was her eyes that

kept straying to him, and he was always with Angélique.
She sat with them to eat steaks and salads and, much
as she wanted to dislike Angélique, she couldn't.

She was pleasant and unpretentious, her voice was soft
and husky, and when Penny spilt some lemonade over
the beautiful ivory silk frock she didn't mind at all. It
was Penny who was stricken. Her animation fled and
she bowed her head. It was Angélique who instantly put
it right by hugging her and saying, 'Don't worry. Your
father's already spilt his drink over me, so I don't see
why you shouldn't.'

She laughed, and Penny's head came up and she
laughed with her. So, Elisa thought, Angélique is good
with children, too. It only reinforced what Anne had
been getting at, that Angélique and Rafe were tailor-
made for each other. As for me, she thought, her heart
twisting in anguish, I just happen to love him, and that
doesn't count at all.

The sun was beginning to set by the time the barbecue
was finished, and everybody began to drift back to the
villa. Elisa took Penny to the bathing cabins and they
changed out of their swimsuits. 'We'll put on our
sweaters, too,' Elisa said. 'It will be getting chilly soon.'

When they had put the beach-bags back into the Land
Rover and climbed the steps to the villa, they found
somebody had put on a stereo and couples were dancing.
Penny ran off to play with the children in the garden
and Elisa had the dubious pleasure of watching Rafe
and Angélique in each other's arms. They talked all the
time as they danced, her face turned up to his, his smiling
down at hers. Elisa would have had to be blind not to
see how close they were, in more ways than one.

The anguish, which didn't lessen with familiarity,
struck once more and stayed with her.

She danced herself, never at a loss for a partner, and she saw that Rafe and Angélique danced with other partners, too. She yearned for Rafe to ask her, knowing that only his arms around her could lull the pain, if only for a few precious minutes. He never did. She laughed and joked and chatted, anything to hide the fact that she was frozen with grief inside.

She never thought that this was worse than she had suffered with Austyn, because he never crossed her mind. One heartbreak was totally eclipsed by another. Her heart was beating for Rafe alone now, but this time she had lost the will-power to save herself, to flee.

Dusk fell and the lights were switched on, making the atmosphere all the more intimate. Elisa discovered hope was a funny thing, and never quite died, because her pulses began racing when she saw Rafe striding purposefully through the throng towards her. So it was going to happen, she was going to be in his arms...

'Time to say goodbye to Anne and collect Penny,' he said. 'We're leaving. She must be falling asleep by now.'

On top of her disappointment, his voice was harsh. Had he found it so very difficult to say goodnight to Angélique? Was he wishing, however fleetingly, that he didn't have a child to drag him away? As for herself, his tone was clear proof she didn't figure in his calculations.

Anne was very friendly towards Elisa, inviting her to visit any time she was at a loose end. 'This beach is always quiet and if I should happen to be out, the maids will make you welcome until I get back. Angélique asked me to say goodbye for her. She's just caught sight of the time and she and the boys are flying back to Athens tonight. The boys have school in the morning.'

So that was why Rafe was disgruntled. Not because he'd had to leave Angélique, but because she'd had to leave him. More for something to say than anything, Elisa remarked, 'They'll be sleepy by the time they get to bed.'

'Oh, no, they live in the Greek style,' Anne replied with a laugh. 'A good siesta, and then up until all hours of the night. It's not a bad way to live once you get used to it.'

They said their goodbyes, found Penny and began the drive home. Penny didn't seem at all tired at first, but the quiet, the motion of the car, soon had her eyes drooping. They stopped to wrap her in a travel rug and lie her down, and she was asleep almost before they set off again.

The silence continued. I must say something, Elisa thought. He might get the idea I'm sulking, and then what will I say? But her mind was numb, perhaps because once more she was having to pretend she wasn't agonisingly aware of his closeness.

It was Rafe who eventually broke the silence. 'You enjoyed yourself.' He made it sound like an accusation.

Elisa was startled. At first she thought only a jealous man could speak like that. Only after frantic thought did another explanation occur to her, and humiliation stained her cheeks. She said stiffly, 'You mean I shouldn't have behaved like a guest? I'm sorry, put it down to inexperience. I'm not used to this sort of work.'

'Don't be ridiculous! I didn't mean that.'

'What did you mean, then?'

'God knows,' he muttered.

'I'm glad somebody does, because I don't,' she grumbled. She'd known him in many moods, but never just plain moody. He didn't seem to know what he was angry about or what to focus it on, and she just happened to be there. Tough luck on her!

The silence was ominous now, and it got to her enough to make her ask, 'Did your business go badly?'

'No.'

That wasn't helpful, and she couldn't believe anything had gone wrong with his personal relationship with Angélique. Besides, Anne wouldn't have been that complacent when they left. What had happened, then, to make him turn on her? She didn't dare ask any more questions, not before his mood softened.

After a while he told her, 'Anyway, I'm glad you enjoyed yourself,' and she knew that was his way of making amends. Whatever the cause of the storm, it had passed. Then he took her aback by asking, 'Is that all Penny and me are to you—work?'

He sounded disgruntled and she asked tremulously, 'Wh-what do you mean?'

'Your stay with us should be something of a holiday as well.'

'Oh. Yes, yes, of course it is.'

He snatched a quick glance at her. 'We'll be doing a fair bit of socialising from now on. I'll give you some expenses to cover suitable clothes.'

Was he ashamed of her well-washed cotton among all that couturier silk? With anybody else, she would have been amused. With Rafe she was so extraordinarily sensitive that her voice trembled with anger as she retorted, 'No, thanks. What I have suits me fine.'

'Don't be so bloody proud. I'm only trying to be nice.'

But Elisa had taken one knock too many. She rounded on him with a viciousness that stunned him. 'Don't try to be nice, Rafe, it would be too much of a shock to both our systems. Be bloody awful, as usual. That way we know just where we are with each other.'

They drove the rest of the way home in frigid, fuming silence.

CHAPTER ELEVEN

FROM the next day on, and purely for Penny's sake, Elisa and Rafe kept up a very good imitation of the companionship they'd lost almost as soon as they'd discovered it. There was a barrier between them neither attempted to cross. It had nothing to do with Angélique, Austyn or anybody else. It was theirs alone, and somehow that made it all the more formidable.

In her wiser moments Elisa wondered if they were both sulking, but she didn't have many wise moments. There was no wisdom—or logic, for that matter—in her love for Rafe and, besides, she didn't believe they could both be guilty of such childishness. They weren't teenagers, for heaven's sake!

No, it was more credible that the moments of closeness they'd shared had been nothing more than a series of illusions, transitory, insubstantial—but deceiving utterly at the time because they'd seemed so real. That was what illusions were all about.

Rafe had always been so wary and unpredictable that, as the days passed, it was difficult for Elisa to detect any actual changes. It was more a matter of the senses. In herself, the changes were more obvious. She had lost her resilience, and with it her ability to seize life with both hands and shake what she could from it.

It was an increasing strain to play herself as she had been—bouncy, rolling with the punch and coming up laughing. If Penny hadn't been a child, she could never have fooled her. As for Rafe—well, when had she ever known what he was thinking?

Having coaxed Penny out of her shell so successfully, she was now shrinking back into hers, which was weird, because she hadn't known she had one. She didn't take up Anne's invitation to visit, and rarely saw her own friends. She wearied of rushing around the island sight-seeing, and more and more she took Penny to the secluded beach where Rafe had kissed her so passionately and selfishly. Penny loved the place, Spiro and Christina spoiled her, and Elisa could torture herself with memories.

Sometimes Rafe would take a few hours off work and he would pick up Penny and drive off with her, just father and daughter with no nanny needed. It was part of the handing-over process so that Penny wouldn't miss Elisa too much when she left. It was sensible, but it hurt. Elisa had become soft and sentimental, and she wanted to be missed.

It seemed as though every day became one more hill to climb, and always with a smiling face, so that life was blurring into one long endurance test. But there were moments that stood out that weren't illusions, they couldn't be because they were all too painfully real.

One was when she did a very silly thing and went into Corfu Town and bought a silk frock, which was what that one-quarrel-too-many had been about in the first place. It was a flamboyant mixture of blues from smoke to indigo, artfully cut so it fell in a slender sheath from narrow shoulder straps until the skirt flared from a dropped waistline.

Elisa tried it on and felt like a million dollars. She could have travelled for weeks, in her frugal way, on what it cost her, but she had to have it. She didn't know why. She had no intention of wearing it for Rafe. But it satisfied some craving within her, and she said to

Penny, 'That's a present from me to me, how about a present from me to you?'

'I'll have an ice-cream,' Penny said, bored. 'I've got enough frocks.'

When they got home, Elisa hung the dress in her wardrobe, shut the door firmly on it and that was that—or so she thought until the following Sunday. Half-way through breakfast, Penny looked at Elisa and said, 'What are we going to do before we go to Aunty Anne's barbecue?'

Elisa carefully avoided Rafe's eyes. She didn't know there was another barbecue, so it was obvious he didn't want her to go. She understood, of course, but that didn't stop the hurt that almost paralysed her throat. After a moment, she replied, 'Just you and Daddy will be going. I'm going to turn that sketch I did of Spiro's beach into a watercolour.'

'Oh, no, Elisa! That's a rainy-day job, you said so yourself. Come with us. It won't be half so much fun without you.' She turned to Rafe. 'You tell her, Daddy, then she'll have to come.'

Elisa's throat constricted again as Rafe replied, 'Elisa deserves some time to herself if she wants it.' There was the proof she wasn't wanted.

'But Elisa wants to come,' Penny protested. 'She's bought a new frock. It's blue and pretty and cost *thousands* and *thousands* of drachmas. That's 'cos it's silk.'

Elisa wanted to die. Rafe must be thinking she was ready to grovel. She could feel the full force of his eyes on her and valiantly fought their magnetism. She must *not* look at him. She really would die if he guessed how she was smarting.

'Did you buy the frock for the barbecue?' he asked intently.

She had all her defensive forces mustered now, and she managed a laugh. 'Heavens, no! Your and my idea of what's right for a barbecue are poles apart. "Nothing that will spoil" you advised me last week, remember? As far as I'm concerned, silk spoils easily.'

'I see.'

No, you don't, you brute, Elisa thought. You don't want me with you, and I'm trying to make it easy for you. If you understood that, you'd drop it.

'What did you buy it for?' he persisted.

'Rich's farewell party,' she lied wildly, not being able to say it had been her soul craving for something lovely. 'Penny and I called at the café for tea this week, and he told us he's flying to Israel to work in a kibbutz. He's finished the Corfu research on his thesis.' That part was true enough, although she'd intended to go in jeans like everybody else.

'When is this party?'

'Next Tuesday week.'

'I don't care about then, what about now? I want you to come with us,' Penny wailed, and burst into tears. They looked at her in consternation. Penny never cried, but then there'd been a time when she'd never laughed, either.

Rafe and Elisa exchanged their first genuine look since their quarrel. 'Tears can be healthy,' she breathed, and then they were both mopping her up and soothing her. Elisa told her hastily, 'It's all right, darling, of course I'll come. I didn't really want to paint, anyway.'

'Th-then why did you s-say you wouldn't come?' Penny hiccuped.

'I'm a girl.' Elisa improvised. 'Sometimes I like to be persuaded.'

'You'll be very welcome,' Rafe said belatedly, but with a stiffness that struck her as insincere. Back to square one, Elisa thought, but she went to the barbecue...in the same cottons. It was an act of defiance, but she needed something to bolster her ego. It was hard to remember she'd once been so bitter about his rough treatment of her. His laboured courtesy seemed so much more of an insult now.

The only difference with Anne's barbecue to the previous week was that the twins were missing. Angélique had left them in Athens with their uncle. She had a full week of business commitments on Corfu, she explained, and she didn't want the boys to miss their schooling.

Elisa guessed the business would be mixed with the pleasure of Rafe's company.

Without Gwen to give a hand with the children, Elisa was busy. She didn't mind that. It was better than watching Angélique and Rafe together all day. She had enough of that when the dancing started after dusk. Elisa danced with whoever asked her, giving an excellent performance of a sought-after girl enjoying herself. When she could, she slipped away to get herself a cool drink and sat on the patio wall to rest her feet. She'd been running around all day.

When she saw Rafe coming towards her she stood up. It was time to go. Unbelievably, his arm went around her waist and he drew her back in among the dancers. They neither spoke nor looked at each other, but their bodies were making love—there was no other way to describe the natural way they moulded together, Elisa thought, trembling between panic and pleasure. It was the pleasure that triumphed and she gave herself up to the bliss of the moment. Her eyes closed, her head rested on his shoulder, and if she only imagined his lips kissing her hair, then so be it. An illusion could be very, very precious.

The music stopped and Rafe put her away from him, deliberately but gently. 'Do you want to finish your drink before we go?'

She shook her head. Funny how, in all the important moments of her life, a chatterbox like herself couldn't speak a word. She couldn't think of much to say on the way home, either. It didn't matter. Penny was awake and talkative. Elisa listened, and wondered why Rafe had asked her to dance. Courtesy, she decided eventually, and wondered if anybody had ever died of kindness.

It couldn't be more than that, because the barrier was still there. Otherwise they'd have plenty to say to each other instead of absolutely nothing at all.

A few days later the fine weather was punctuated by intermittent torrential downpours. The morning had been fine enough, but by midday Elisa and Penny fled from Spiro's beach back to the villa. They changed into their 'heavy duty' clothes—jeans and jumpers—and Elisa lit the fire in the sitting-room. They had toasted bacon sandwiches and fruit for lunch, then they sprawled on the thick-pile rug in front of the fire and played Ludo, snakes and ladders, and any other game Penny fancied.

She wasn't a difficult child to entertain, and the afternoon passed pleasantly enough. There were sunny spells between the rain, but they weren't bored enough to go out of doors. A couple of hours before Rafe was due home they were both stretched out on the floor on their tummies, their fair heads close together as they studied the same book.

The rain was lashing down again and Elisa said, 'Next time it stops we'll jump into the car and dash down to Rich's for dinner. We'll play safe and eat in the hotel, not the beach café. That thatched roof looks pretty, but it leaks.'

'Um,' Penny replied absently, writing with painstaking care on a pad. 'Where's "D"?'

Elisa studied the book and pointed. 'There.' Penny wrote on and Elisa looked out of the french windows. The rain was drumming down with such force, it was hitting the patio and bouncing up again.

Penny pushed the pad towards Elisa and asked, 'Have I got it right?'

Elisa compared the lettering with the book. 'Yes.' She dropped a kiss on the curly head. 'Clever you.' She didn't know what made her look round then, it just seemed instinct. Rafe stood there studying them, how long he'd been there, she didn't know. 'Hello,' she said. 'We didn't hear you come in. The rain must have drowned the sound of the car.' And she thought sadly, When I speak to you now it's only to say stupid things. Where did the laughter go, and the quarrels? Anything is better than this.

Penny had jumped up and launched herself at her father. He picked her up, carried her to the armchair by the fire and sat with her on his knee. 'What were you two so engrossed with when I came in?'

Penny wiggled her fingers excitedly at Elisa, who gave her the pad. She held it for her father to see. 'Hello, Daddy,' he read.

'We got it right!' Penny exclaimed, and explained in a rush, 'Elisa and I are learning the Greek alphabet.'

'Yes, and she's learning quicker than I am. It's humiliating,' Elisa said ruefully, beginning to tidy up the clutter on the floor, 'and very slovenly we've been about it, by the looks of things.'

Penny went rigid on Rafe's knee. 'Not *slovenly*,' she whispered, 'that's a very bad thing to be. It means lazy and careless and untidy.'

Thank you, Janet Tilson, Elisa thought, because she hadn't seen that stricken look on Penny's face for a long time. 'Slovenly is only bad if you're like it *all* the time. Lazy and untidy some of the time just means you're relaxed, and that's good.'

'Oh,' Penny said dubiously.

Rafe fished in his pocket and brought out a set of photographs. 'Look, Penny, what do you think of these?'

Penny exclaimed and laughed over them, and passed them on to Elisa one by one. They were from that magical Saturday when she'd thought she and Rafe were forging links that couldn't easily be broken. How wrong she'd been! There were shots of her and Penny, Rafe and Penny, and one of herself Rafe must have taken without her knowing. How happy she looked.

The last photograph almost stopped her heart. It was of her and Rafe, and Penny had made a good job of it. Rafe had his arm around her shoulder, she was leaning against him, and Penny must have closed the shutter a second before they were ready, because they were smiling at each other and not the camera.

She tried not to look at the photograph too long, and as she gave the set back to Rafe, she asked, 'May I borrow the negatives? I'd like to get some copies.'

'That's your set. I ordered two.'

'Thank you.' She stretched across to put some of the tidied boxes of games beside the photographs he'd put on a side table, and began gathering the rest of the clutter.

'I came home early because I have some work to clear up,' he went on. 'I'm flying to London first thing in the morning. Angélique has a business meeting there, and she's going by private charter. There's a spare seat and I thought I'd grab it to——'

That was as far as he got before Penny clutched his shirt and cried, 'Are you taking me with you?'

'No, you'll be staying with Elisa. I'll——'

Penny jumped off his knee and hurled herself at Elisa, beating at her with little hands curled into fists. 'It's all your fault!' she stormed, as Elisa, kneeling on the floor and taken by surprise, reeled back under the onslaught. 'You made me untidy. You said it didn't matter. But it did, it did! Daddy's leaving me and it's all your fault.'

'Penny!' Rafe snatched Penny away from Elisa, and the little girl collapsed into hysterical tears. He sat down with her, cradled her in his arms and soothed, 'Ssh, darling, you didn't give me chance to explain...'

Elisa picked herself up from the floor and sat in the opposite armchair. Rafe's eyes met hers and he asked, 'Are you all right?'

She was shaken, but she nodded. 'Let her cry it all out of her. Her fears have been pent up too long.'

Penny cried for a long time, but when her sobs began to subside Rafe told her softly, 'I'm only going for one day. I'm flying out at dawn and I'm coming back in the evening. You might be in bed by then, but I'll be here when you wake up the next morning. I don't *want* to go, but I have to see Miss Tilson. There are some things I have to settle up with her. You see, she won't be looking after you any more.'

Penny lifted her tear-stained face from his shoulder and said tremulously, 'B-but she helps me stay quiet and clean and tidy so you won't get fed up with me and go away and leave me as Mummy always did.'

Rafe looked away from Penny for a moment, and Elisa knew it was to master his rage. He succeeded, because his voice was soft when he looked back and asked, 'Did Miss Tilson tell you that?'

When Penny nodded, he told her, 'She was wrong. You're my little girl and I love you. It doesn't matter if you're clean, dirty, noisy or quiet, I'd still love you. All I care about is that you're happy, comfortable—and yourself. That's what's important, Penny Sinclair just as she is.'

He kissed her cheek and received a fervent hug in return, and she mumbled into his neck, 'You won't go away for ever and ever, no matter what I do?'

'You've got it,' he said, ruffling her hair. 'Any trips I make will be business trips, and they'll be short. You'll know exactly why I'm away, and I'll phone you every day until I get back. All right?'

'All right.' Penny nodded with the beginnings of a smile.

Elisa relaxed. It was going to be all right. She crept away and came back with a flannel and a towel. She knelt beside the armchair to wash Penny's face, and told her, 'You listen to Daddy, and I'll go and make some tea.'

Penny disentangled her arms from Rafe's neck and hugged Elisa. 'I'm sorry. I didn't mean to hurt you. I was just so frightened.'

'I know. If I was a little girl, I dare say I'd have done the same thing. Are you hungry?'

Penny said she was and Elisa said to Rafe, 'We were just going out to eat when you came home, but I think it would be better if we stayed in this evening. I could throw together a glorified mixed grill, if that's all right?'

'Please,' they both said together.

Elisa smiled, cleared the things off the side table and a few minutes later she put a tea tray beside them. She drank her tea in the kitchen while she prepared the meal. She didn't hurry. Penny's fears were out in the open now, and Rafe had proved he could deal with them. Father and daughter were talking as they never had before, and she allowed them all the time they needed.

When the meal was nearly ready, she went into the sitting-room and asked, 'What say we eat our meal hippy style, on our laps in front of the fire?'

Penny looked anxiously at her father for his approval, making Elisa realise it would be a long time before she overcame all of her anxiety, saw his smile and replied, 'Please! It'll be as much fun as going out for breakfast.'

The novelty of eating in front of the fire cheered up Penny. Her emotional outburst had taken its toll, though, and she was so weary when they'd finished that Elisa prepared her for bed. Rafe had taken over reading the bedtime story, so while he was upstairs Elisa cleared away the dishes.

She was curled up in the fireside chair when he came down again. He said as he sat opposite her, 'She's fast asleep. I know that outburst was what she needed, but I'm sorry you bore the brunt of it. You seem to bear the brunt of everything, including my bad temper. You must be sick of the Sinclairs.'

'I can be pretty fiery myself,' Elisa reminded him. 'Was it Janet who discouraged Penny from playing with other children?'

'Yes, on the grounds it would make her noisy and untidy, and I'd be angry. I won't rest until I've had it out with Janet. She must be sick in the head. She damned nearly destroyed my child.'

'How old is Janet?'

'Thirty-five.'

'She might be more selfish than sick. Penny's rapidly outgrowing the need for a nanny, and I suppose she didn't fancy starting all over again with a new family. While she could keep Penny alienated from you and dependent on her, she could be sure of keeping her job. You offer a life-style that's hard to beat, Rafe, and with a child frightened into docility she had hardly anything to do.'

'Janet knew Penny was already stricken by Sheena's indifference and spite, so she had easy material to work on, hadn't she? My God, I could murder the woman!'

His expression frightened Elisa, and she said hastily, 'Losing your temper won't do any good.'

'It will make me feel better,' snarled Rafe.

'Just get rid of her. You've been saying for a while that you have your daughter back—well, now it's really true. Penny went into a flat panic when she thought you were leaving her, but it didn't affect her priorities. It wasn't you she turned on, it was me. She was protecting what was most precious to her, just as she's been trying to all along. She was never frightened *of* you, but of losing you. She made it pretty clear I'm the expendable one, which is as it should be.'

'You know, Elisa,' Rafe said softly, 'you're quite a girl. Penny's always known it, right from the start. There's nothing wrong with her instincts. It was mine that were all screwed up. Under any circumstances I wouldn't call you expendable.'

She had always yearned for his appreciation. Now, perversely, she couldn't accept it. 'Nonsense. The trick was in getting Janet out of the way, and that was already done when I came on the scene.'

'The trick,' he contradicted, and with such tenderness her heart began to thump erratically, 'was in getting you here. Not anybody, but you. You have a special touch, a way of——'

He broke off, and the way he was staring at her made Elisa catch her breath...and lose her fear of being duped into a new feeling of closeness. Her guard was down, but his? She knew it was still up when he looked away from her and gazed into the fire. She had lost him again, and she didn't know why. Yes, of course she did. Angélique! There'd been too much emotion in this room tonight. It was spilling over into all the wrong places.

Rafe must have thought so, too. He never finished what he was about to say, but harked back to something he'd said earlier, a ploy to get himself out of an awkward situation. Elisa was sure of that, because it was a rather heavy-handed attempt to tease her. 'When I mentioned what I'd like to do to Janet, you didn't think I was really capable of murder, did you?'

'I hope not. I've been a substitute target once tonight. I don't fancy going another round.'

She meant it as a joke, but it came out resentful. Rafe stood up in that angrily abrupt way of his that made her feel so rejected. 'You have nothing to fear from me. I made that plain the day I brought you here. Now, if you'll excuse me, I have that work to catch up on. I'm leaving before dawn. I should be back by eight tomorrow evening at the latest. Goodnight, Elisa.'

'Goodnight.' Dully she watched him walk into the study and close the door. She was shut out again, and she thought she should be in the *Guinness Book of Records* as the girl who never learned.

CHAPTER TWELVE

BREAKFAST without Rafe gave Elisa an insight into how life would be when she left the villa. Empty. There would be more than an ache in her heart as there had been when she'd run away from Austyn; there would be a huge gap nothing would ever fill. She must have been in love with love itself when she'd fallen for Austyn. With Rafe, she was in love with a man. No doubt about that.

Left to herself, she would have moped about the house all day until he came home, because that was where she felt closest to him, but that wouldn't do. Penny was none too perky, either, so they went for a drive and ended up on Spiro's beach, which was the next best thing.

Elisa intended to stay there until late, but by mid-afternoon Penny began to get restless. Her anxiety that Rafe wouldn't return was coming back to her. Frantic for something to reassure her, Elisa suggested, 'Why don't we drive into town and buy a lot of goodies for a surprise supper for Daddy, in case he's hungry when he gets home?'

As an idea it was an inspiration. Penny bubbled over with enthusiasm. They bought green and ripe black olives, anchovies, tiny pies stuffed with feta cheese, crisps, and the ingredients for snacks they could make themselves. When they got home, Penny stood on a stool by a kitchen counter and helped Elisa prepare vine leaves stuffed with savoury rice, little meatballs, a creamy fish roe paste to spread on crispy bread, a cheese dip and small pieces of sausage speared with cocktail sticks.

It took Penny's mind completely off her anxiety, and even helped Elisa forget for minutes at a time that Rafe was with Angélique. Had she really had business in London, or had they gone together to confront Janet? If Angélique was to become Penny's mother, she had a vested interest. Reason told Elisa that Rafe had no reason to be secretive about his plans with Angélique, but then, he wasn't naturally a communicative man and there was no reason why he should tell her, either.

All in all, she was as glad as Penny to have something to keep her busy. It was gone seven by the time the little feast was set out under cling-film on the sitting-room table. Elisa added the decanter of brandy for Rafe, lemonade for Penny and prepared fresh coffee. There was nothing to do after that but wait. They were still waiting at half-past eight.

'He's not coming home,' Penny said, her soft mouth drooping.

'Yes, he is. I expect his flight was delayed. It happens all the time.' Having told Penny what she'd been telling herself, Elisa continued, 'Shall we start the feast by ourselves?'

Penny shook her head. Tears, Elisa suspected, weren't far away. 'I know,' she said, 'let's get you ready for bed. Once you're in your pyjamas and dressing-gown, you can sit up with me until Daddy comes home.'

'All night?'

'If necessary.' Elisa thought if she could get Penny curled up comfortably in one of the fireside chairs she would fall asleep soon enough. She was wrong. By ten o'clock the sitting-room floor was littered with discarded games and toys, Penny was sitting wide awake and anxious on Elisa's knee, and Elisa's voice was husky from reading stories to her.

It was so quiet up in the hills that they heard the Land Rover before it turned off the road on to the track. They both jumped up, as excited as two-year-olds, and scrabbled around, frantically whipping the covers off the food and making the floor look tidier by the simple means of pushing everything into one big pile. Then Penny grabbed Elisa's hand and pulled her to the front door.

They opened it as Rafe was getting out of the car, light streaming towards him and showing his surprised expression. Penny hurled herself into his arms and clung to his neck. 'You came home!' she cried, but she was laughing excitedly, not crying.

'Of course I did,' he said, kissing her. 'The flight was delayed because of an air traffic controllers' dispute, but never mind about that now. This is what I call a welcome.'

'There's more inside,' Penny told him. 'We made a feast, Elisa and me, and we haven't touched it although we're starving. We waited for you because it's *your* feast.'

'Lead me to it, I'm also starving.' Rafe's eyes were on Elisa. The way Penny was clinging to him told its own story, and he asked softly, 'Had a harrowing time?'

Elisa shook her head, but he didn't believe her. He kissed her on the cheek and put an arm around her shoulders as they went back into the house. He could be so affectionate, so understanding, and so lovable when the mood took him, she thought wistfully.

Rafe stood still when he saw the 'feast'. 'It's all fresh,' Penny told him eagerly. 'We cooked for *hours* and it's been ready for *ages*, but we didn't unwrap it until we heard the car.'

'You make me feel more than welcome,' Rafe said, 'you make me feel special.'

'Well, you are,' Penny told him. 'You're my daddy.'

Elisa slipped away into the kitchen to make coffee. She was just pouring it when Rafe's arms came around her waist from behind. 'Thank you,' he said. She felt his lips on her hair, her cheek and her neck, and then he was gone.

She was unable to move for a minute, fighting off the urge to burst into tears. Oh, gosh, he had made her feel special, too. How like the man, she thought, to come along and break her into little pieces just when she thought she was doing a good job of getting herself together again.

They all ate in front of the fire. They talked and they laughed, and then Penny fell asleep on Rafe's lap. He carried her up to bed, and Elisa carried the plates into the kitchen. Rafe came down and ordered her out of there. 'What do you think I employ a housekeeper for? Anyway, it's all right to be slovenly sometimes. You said so yourself.'

In the sitting-room he poured her a glass of brandy and asked, 'What do you want to ruin it with this time?'

'Cola, please. It makes it into a long, cool sundowner.'

Rafe looked heavenwards in despair, but he did as she asked. He's happy, she thought, and that makes me happy. Paradise was made for fools like me, it's the place you get kicked out of...

If she had to leave, she was glad it would be before the evenings up here in the hills became warm enough to make a fire superfluous. Of the many ways she would remember Rafe, this would be the sweetest. The evening quiet of this dimly lit room, the two armchairs, the glow of the fire on his face, his voice...

She could scarcely bear the sweetness now, while she was still with him, and to divert her mind from the sad prospects of the future, she asked, 'How did you get on with Janet?'

'Mmm?' Rafe looked at her vaguely, as though his mind had been on something else. 'Oh, Janet. She was a very cold, calculating bitch to the last. She said Penny had been telling stories. When I pointed out that Penny didn't really need to say anything, because the difference in her under your care told its own story, she refused to talk at all.'

'What did you do?'

'I paid her off. Physically she's well. In fact, she was going to fly back here at the end of the week. Now she's going to her mother's. I told her I wanted her out of my house by the end of the week. The housekeeper can send her things on if necessary. That's Penny's home as well as mine, and I can't bear to think of that creature there one moment longer than she has to be.'

'So it's over.'

'Yes.'

They were silent for a while, then Rafe told her, 'There'll be some disruption next week. I'm having men in to re-paint the villa white.'

'I'm glad about that.' But she was thinking: Sheena's gone, Janet's gone, I'm next. The way is clear for Angélique. Or was this place to be sold and the villa he was designing for Angélique really for both of them?

'When's Rich's farewell party?' he asked suddenly.

'Tuesday evening. You won't need me then, will you?'

'How will you get there and back?'

'I'll drive,' Elisa replied, surprised he was interested.

'On these roads, after you've been drinking? I could pick you up if you liked.'

'Oh.' She was touched by his offer, but she had to refuse it. She couldn't put herself in a situation with him where she might lose control. 'I can take or leave alcohol, and on Tuesday I'll leave it. I just want to say goodbye to Rich, and to my other friends as well. I'm off myself on Saturday.'

Rafe picked up a log, turned it in his hands as though he were considering something, then put it on the fire. 'You don't have to go. In fact, now you haven't a travelling companion, there's no reason why you shouldn't stay.'

Elisa could think of several. She was terrified of revealing her love for him. It was all pent up inside her, like a steam kettle just needing a mite more pressure to blow the lid right off. And, worse than that, she couldn't go on watching him with Angélique, she just couldn't.

'Well, Elisa?' he asked.

She watched the flames lick round the fresh log, anything rather than look at him. 'Babs has a new travelling partner lined up for me. I'll meet her when I go to Athens, and take it from there. Besides, it wouldn't be good for Penny if I stayed any longer. She's an affectionate child. I don't want her getting unduly attached to me.'

'You don't want to stay,' he said flatly.

'No.' She put down her glass and stood up. 'It's been a long day. Goodnight, Rafe.'

'Goodnight.'

It was the first time she'd broken up one of their fireside chats, and it took all her will-power. She couldn't even console herself that he was suffering the rejection she always felt when he walked away from her.

Tuesday evening, Elisa pinned her hair on top of her head, wore her silk dress with its myriad shades of blue, ruined the effect by putting a denim jacket over it, and drove down to the party. It really didn't matter what she looked like, because Rafe hadn't been there to see it.

He'd taken Penny over to Anne's for the afternoon and hadn't returned.

The party was a good one, and she was as miserable as sin.

When she was dancing with Rich, he said, 'This is your last chance to tell me why you really became a vagabond for a year.'

Why not? she thought. Austyn didn't hurt any more. 'I fell in love with a married man, an old problem you must have heard a million times before. I was looking for a cure.'

'Have you found it?'

'Yes.'

'You could have fooled me. I've never known you so quiet.'

'I'll liven up later,' Elisa assured him, smiling beautifully, but without her usual brilliance. 'I've been leading such a staid life lately, it's taking me a while to loosen up.'

But she never did loosen up. She spent a lot of time with Sue, who was in floods of tears because Rich was leaving and she'd failed to push their relationship beyond the friendship stage. Sue's heart broke and mended easily, but Elisa felt honour-bound to console her, even though she was certain her own heartbreak would never mend.

They walked back and forth along the beach, talking. Privately Elisa wondered how Sue would cope if she ever fell truly in love. That wasn't all she wondered about, either. Her mind kept going back to Rafe's offer to pick her up tonight. Had he merely been concerned for an employee, or worried about her, Elisa? And had he really wanted her to stay on at the villa because he would miss her, or merely to keep things running smoothly until Angélique took over, as she surely would?

I'll never make a *femme fatale*, she mused. I miss all my chances. I can't seize what little Rafe offers and make the most of it. I suppose it's because I know if I don't walk away from him, then he'll walk away from me. I suppose everybody has something they can't face up to...

Somewhere around eleven o'clock, Sue stopped crying. She rejoined the party and Elisa left it. Unable to laugh, unable to cry, she was prey to a terrible kind of anguish as she drove home. All the downstairs lights were on at the villa, streaming across the patios and loggias like a homing beacon.

So Rafe was still up. She didn't want to see him. If she did, she had the awful feeling she would walk straight into his arms, bury her face in his chest and say, Love me, even if it's only tonight.

The lid was coming off the steam kettle. She just wasn't *safe*.

Elisa parked at the side of the house. She could hear music. Something by Ravel. Moody, passionate, inspiring. The last thing she needed. She hoped it would cover the sound of her arrival, and let herself quietly in the front door. It wasn't as if Rafe was sitting up for her, he wouldn't be listening.

Elisa crossed the hall and was two or three steps up the stairs when Rafe came out of the sitting-room. He was wearing white trousers, a blue shirt, his eyes were not like ice and she almost died of love for him. She paused as he came towards her and asked, 'Were you going to bed without saying goodnight?'

'I didn't want to disturb you.'

'I could do with some company. I can't offer you a feast, but there's a fire and a drink.' Her hand was on the banister and he covered it with his. 'You're cold.'

Elisa's heart began to hammer. He hadn't taken his hand away. She thought: Don't do this to me, Rafe.

Don't flirt with me and make me happy, and then, just when I begin to believe in it, leave me cold. She slipped her hand from under his and hoped her smile was as deceitful as it was meant to be. 'I'll soon warm up under the shower, thanks all the same. I'm tired.'

'Wasn't it a good party?'

'Fine, but it's a bit dreary to keep saying goodbye. Enough is enough.'

Rafe's eyes went slowly over her. 'I'm surprised you were allowed to leave. I've never seen you looking more beautiful.'

He *was* flirting with her, damn him. He was playing a game while she was dying... 'Thank you,' she replied, 'but frankly I was overdressed among all that denim.'

'No, you're never over or underdressed, because you have a marvellous capacity for making everybody else look wrong. When I asked if you needed new clothes, I wasn't being critical, I thought *you* might want them. Sometimes I'm clumsy when I try to be nice. Out of practice, I suppose.'

'Oh.' She wished he would stop it. It would be so fatally easy to forget about Angélique, forget about everything... 'Well, what I want doesn't usually come into it. I'm limited to what I can carry in my backpack.'

'Yet you bought that dress for Rich's party.' It was another of his accusations, and a jealous one.

It couldn't be. Once or twice before she'd thought he'd been jealous, but she'd always been proved wrong. Suddenly she knew she couldn't take any more. She had to get away from him before her head started believing what her heart wanted to believe. 'I bought it for *myself*. I'm a woman. I get these irresistible impulses sometimes. Goodnight, Rafe.' And she fled up the stairs.

Elisa showered, brushed her hair and put on an old cotton button-through shirt that doubled as a nightshirt.

She slipped her feet into sandals in lieu of slippers, and prowled restlessly about the room. She wasn't cold now. The heat of the day seemed to be trapped in this sunny room and, besides, she was burning with emotion.

Rafe's music stopped. She heard him come upstairs, shower and go to his room at the other end of the passage. Perhaps this was what she'd been waiting for, knowing he was safely penned for the night, before going to sleep. She was turning down the covers on her bed when she remembered she hadn't looked in on Penny. It wasn't really necessary, but it was a habit she'd fallen into and habits were hard to break.

Penny's room was next to hers. Elisa went in. The curtains weren't drawn to, and there was enough moonlight to show her the bed was empty. She switched on the light to be sure, searched the bathroom, then ran along the passage to Rafe's door. The light was shining beneath it. She knocked hastily and rushed in.

Rafe was coming towards the door, and she almost fell into his arms. He was wearing a white towelling robe, his hair was still damp from his shower and he threw the book he was holding aside as he caught her. 'Penny's missing!' she burst out. 'She's not in her bed or the bathroom or——'

'She's at Anne's,' he told her. 'She fell asleep, so Anne put her to bed. She'll be all right. I'll go over to pick her up first thing. Anne has other guests. I didn't want to crowd her out so I came home.'

'Oh.' Of course it had to be something like that. 'I'm sorry I disturbed you.'

Rafe looked at her gleaming hair, her softly parted lips, her flushed cheeks and the thin shirt that teasingly revealed and concealed. He said none too steadily, 'You've disturbed me ever since I first set eyes on you.

I don't think I can let you go. You'd better make a run for it.'

But Elisa was looking into his eyes. Unbelievably, they were like lover's eyes. Her legs went weak. She couldn't move.

Rafe drew her towards him, slowly, still giving her the chance to break away. Then she was against his chest, his arms strengthened around her and the chance was lost. The touch of his body against hers eased the ache she had suffered from for so long, and she clung to him shamelessly.

His hand caressed her hair, slid sensuously down her neck and pushed the shirt off her shoulder. He kissed the exposed flesh and Elisa shuddered with ecstasy. The shudder communicated itself to him and he seized her up in his arms and carried her to the bed. He laid her down and lay over her, showering passionate kisses over her face and neck.

Finally, when Elisa felt she could stand no more, he claimed her lips. It was bliss, such insatiable bliss, she was sure they were exchanging souls. Tears trickled from under her closed eyelids. Pride, fear, reserve—all were gone, swept away on the tide of mounting passion. She felt as though they were melting into each other and she asked for nothing more.

Elisa didn't feel him unbuttoning her shirt, but she felt him lift her as he pulled it from her. His robe was gone, she wasn't sure when, but her naked body was clasped to his and she gasped with pleasure. He was murmuring her name over and over again, and she didn't think there was one inch of her he left unkissed or uncaressed.

'Rafe,' she murmured, not knowing whether she was begging or demanding as wave after mounting wave of passion washed over her. 'Rafe...'

When he thrust into her she cried out, she couldn't help it, and he paused and stared at her. 'Elisa...'

She didn't want him to stop. Her arms slipped urgently down his back, urging him on. He thrust again, more violently than he intended, and she felt the pain and then the pleasure of possession.

He kissed her again all over her face and neck, hot, frantic kisses that seared her flesh wherever they fell. Then his urgency could no longer be contained and he begged, 'Move with me, Elisa. Move with me...'

She did as she was told, and with the physical pleasure she felt the spiritual joy of belonging to the man she loved. She cried again, silent tears of supreme happiness, and when he gave a great cry and collapsed against her she held him fiercely, as though guarding this man of hers in his moment of weakness. Now she knew what it was to be a woman. She asked for nothing more.

As their breathing returned to normal, he raised his head and kissed her lips tenderly. 'It will get better for you,' he said. 'Every time will get better.'

He seemed anxious, and she couldn't understand that. She hadn't wanted the moon alone, she'd wanted the stars as well, and he had given them to her. 'It couldn't,' she breathed. 'That was perfect, all I ever dreamed...'

'Why didn't you tell me you...' he began, but she stopped him by pressing her fingers against his lips.

'We don't need words tonight,' she told him, wanting him to understand that the afterglow of their love surpassed the need to communicate in any other way.

Rafe must have understood because he smiled, lay beside her and pulled her into his arms. There she fell asleep, at peace with the world, because her world was him and him alone. Tonight, anyway, and she couldn't—wouldn't!—see beyond tonight.

Elisa woke alone. She woke to many things. The greyness of dawn, the absence of Rafe, uncertainty, the grim reality of her very first thought—that, where she was his alone, she shared him with Angélique. She had to face up to the fact that what had been the summit of her life so far might only have been a passing pleasure for him. What happened now would be entirely up to Rafe. She wouldn't demand or expect anything.

Elisa showered, dressed in shorts and shirt, and stared at herself in the mirror. She wasn't sure what she saw there. Radiance, anxiety—a mixture of the two?

Taking a deep breath, and trying to behave as though this were just another morning, she went down to the kitchen. Rafe was leaning against a kitchen counter, dressed in jeans and short-sleeved, open-necked shirt, drinking the last of his coffee. His car keys were in his hand. She remembered then that he had to go pick up Penny.

If he'd come towards her, she'd have known everything was all right. He didn't. He put down his cup, straightened up. He looked awkward, and Rafe never looked awkward. My God, he was sorry, and he mustn't be sorry. That would spoil everything.

His first words confirmed her worst fears. 'Elisa, I'm sorry, I didn't mean last night to happen. I feel as guilty as hell. I said you'd be safe with me and I seduced you.'

Elisa walked over to the coffee-pot and poured herself a cup. Her legs felt stiff, her face felt stiff with the effort of not showing what she was feeling. 'It takes two, and I was willing.' She tried to sip her coffee, as though that was all there was to it, but she had to keep her back to him.

Rafe came over and touched her shoulder. His hesitancy made her cringe. 'You don't understand,' he told her. 'I've wanted you from the beginning. That's why I was so mad at you half the time. I thought I could hold out until Saturday when you left my employ. I should have known I couldn't. I'm the one with all the experience. You had none at all.'

She wished he'd come straight out with what was really bothering him, that she belonged to last night—and today and tomorrow belonged to Angélique. There was a simple way to tell her. Somehow, she hadn't thought Rafe would dodge an issue like that. He'd spoken his mind enough in the past, and he wasn't short of integrity.

Gently he turned her round to face him. 'Elisa, Penny needs a mother and I need a wife. Would you marry me?'

That was his integrity speaking. He felt he owed her something. She wanted to scream at him that she wanted a lover, not a human sacrifice. How long would it be before he realised she'd done exactly what Sheena had done, and separated him from Angélique? How long before the bitterness and resentment re-emerged? How could she do that to him? If she loved him a little less, perhaps, but—— She twisted out of his arms and moved away from him. 'Angélique is better qualified for that role than I am.'

'Angélique?' He looked stunned. Had he really supposed she hadn't known about her?

'Yes, Angélique,' she repeated, 'and you can stop feeling guilty about me. You see, I wasn't really making love to you at all last night. I was making love to Austyn. In my mind. There was never the opportunity with him. It was only a matter of time before I found the right substitute—you. I'm grateful and not sorry for a thing, so there's no reason for you to be.'

Elisa watched his face whiten. His ego was hurting, but when his fury passed he'd realise he was free. She hadn't mucked up his life. She couldn't do any more for him than that.

'You bitch,' he breathed, and he walked out on her, just as she knew he would.

She heard the Land Rover start up, heard it rev furiously along the track and followed the sound up to the road and beyond until it faded into nothing.

Nothing, which was precisely what she had.

Elisa felt sick. She ran water into the bowl, splashed it up into her face and she still felt sick. She would pack and she would leave. She would leave a note telling him where to find the car, and he would think up a plausible explanation for Penny. But first she'd go out and get some fresh air. This house was claustrophobic. Rafe was everywhere she looked.

She walked outside and looked at her watch. Rafe would be over an hour at the very least—the way he was feeling, he might be all day—but the workmen had started preparing the villa for re-painting and they would be here soon. Elisa sat on a chair under one of the loggias and rested her hot forehead against one of the cool supporting pillars. She was racked with dry, tearless sobs.

She was so deep in misery, she didn't hear the sound of an engine until the Land Rover forced itself into her attention by braking hard in front of the house. She looked up, saw Rafe jump out, and fled through the olive groves in mindless panic. She didn't know what had brought him back, she only knew she couldn't face him.

It never crossed her mind he would follow her, until she heard him pounding behind her. She gave a frightened glance back and saw him catching up fast. She couldn't outrun him. She stopped and turned to face him. 'What do you want?'

He stopped running, but stalked grimly up to her. 'I'm going to make love to you,' he told her savagely, 'and I'm going to keep on making love to you until you know exactly *who* is making love to you. *Me!*'

'Rafe, don't,' she begged, backing away.

He grabbed her and pulled her against him. He twisted a hand into her hair and pulled her head back until she was looking up at him. He looked at her long and hard, then he kissed her. Fiercely, provocatively, demanding a response she couldn't fail to give.

He raised his head and asked, 'Now who kissed you?'

'You,' she whispered.

'Say my name. Say it, damn you.'

'Rafe.' She started to cry.

'Don't think tears will save you,' he said in that same savage tone. He released her hair and his hand slid down her neck and shoulders to her breast. 'Who's touching you?' he demanded. 'Who?'

'You . . . Rafe.' She felt his hand on the buttons of her shirt and whimpered, 'Don't.'

'Christ, you hurt me! And now all you can say is "Don't".' He grasped her shoulders and shook her. 'What's the matter, don't I remind you of your precious Austyn any more?'

'Y-you n-never did,' she stuttered. 'I m-made that up because you h-hurt me with all t-that talk about b-being Penny's mother and y-your wife, but n-never a word about l-loving me.'

His expression changed and he stared at her. 'Not loving you? Do you think I could have made love to you like that last night and *not* love you? I've been going out of my mind with love for you. Why the hell do you think I kept walking away from you? I forced you here, I promised you'd be safe. I couldn't very well seduce you, could I? Then last night——'

Rafe took a shuddering breath and went on more calmly, 'Last night I couldn't walk away. This morning I thought a girl who's waited twenty-five years to make love was waiting until she was married. I thought I'd over-persuaded you and that you might hate me for it. If I said all the wrong things, if I was clumsy, it was because I was scared stiff of losing you. But frankly, Elisa, it never crossed my mind you didn't know I loved you. I thought that had been painfully obvious for weeks. It has been to me.'

'Oh.' Elisa reached blindly for him, buried her face in his shoulder and sobbed in earnest. He picked her up, sat down with his back to an olive tree and cradled her in his arms. He kissed whatever parts of her he could reach, murmuring his love for her until her sobs began to subside.

Then he prised her face out of his shoulder, found a handkerchief, wiped her eyes and told her to blow her nose. 'I love your indigo eyes,' he told her softly. 'I've always thought of them as deep-water eyes, but I've had enough of seeing them at flood-tide. Smile for me, Elisa.'

'I can't. I must look terrible.'

'You do, and I love you.'

Tears welled up again and he hastily kissed them away. 'That's better,' he approved when she smiled tremulously at him, 'now you can tell me why you wanted me to marry Angélique.'

'I thought you wanted to marry her. Anne told me how Sheena broke you up once, and I thought you'd hate me if I did it a second time.'

'Elisa, if I'd ever loved Angélique, nobody could have broken us up. We're very good friends, we're close, but that special something has always been missing.' He kissed her lingeringly and explained, 'That sort of special something. Anne looked on us as an ideal couple, but Angélique and I knew it would never work out. What about you and Austyn?'

'I haven't thought of him for weeks, and when I did it was to realise I never really loved him. I was never out of control, the way I am with you. I'm sorry I cried so much. My heart was breaking——'

'No, it wasn't,' he broke in, 'it was mending just like mine.'

'Rafe, if you don't stop being nice to me, I shall start crying again,' she threatened.

He kissed her nose. 'You cry when I'm nasty, you cry when I'm nice. I can't win, can I?'

'It's not funny. I was going to run away. I didn't think you'd come back. I was so sure you'd never want to see me again.'

'It was fear of that,' he told her tenderly, 'that brought me back. Mad as I was, I couldn't bear the thought of losing you, and fear brings out the worst in me. If I was going to suffer, I was going to make damn sure you suffered with me. Not a very nice character, am I?'

'No, horrible,' Elisa agreed lovingly. 'I thought you were going to murder me.'

'That, too. Whatever it took to keep you with me.' He was bending to kiss her, but the sound of a lorry arriving at the villa made him look up. 'The workmen,' he said, 'and much as I'd like to stay here all day, we have to pick up Penny. I don't want two neurotic females weeping all over me.'

'We're not neurotic. We just need to know we're loved.'

Rafe looked at her seriously, his blue eyes unsmiling. 'You are.'

'So are you,' Elisa whispered. 'So much...'

Harlequin Presents

Coming Next Month

Available in February wherever paperback books are sold, or through
Harlequin Reader Service:

In the U.S.
901 Fuhrmann Blvd.
P.O. Box 1397
Buffalo, N.Y. 14240-1397

In Canada
P.O. Box 603
Fort Erie, Ontario
L2A 5X3

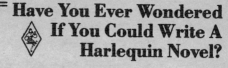

Have You Ever Wondered
If You Could Write A
Harlequin Novel?

Here's great news—Harlequin
is offering a series of cassette
tapes to help you do just that.
Written by Harlequin editors,
these tapes give practical
advice on how to make your
characters—and your story—
come alive. There's a tape for
each contemporary romance
series Harlequin publishes.

Mail order only

All sales final

TO: ***Harlequin Reader Service***
Audiocassette Tape Offer
P.O. Box 1396
Buffalo, NY 14269-1396

I enclose a check/money order payable to HARLEQUIN READER
SERVICE® for $9.70 ($8.95 plus 75¢ postage and handling) for
EACH tape ordered for the total sum of $_____*
Please send:

☐ Romance and Presents   ☐ Intrigue
☐ American Romance   ☐ Temptation
☐ Superromance   ☐ All five tapes ($38.80 total)

Signature_____
                                         (please print clearly)
Name:_____
Address:_____
State:_____ Zip:_____

*Iowa and New York residents add appropriate sales tax.

                                              AUDIO-H

**A compelling novel of deadly revenge and passion
from Harlequin's bestselling international
romance author Penny Jordan**

POWER PLAY

Eleven years had passed but the
terror of that night was something
Pepper Minesse would never
forget. Fueled by revenge against
the four men who had brutally
shattered her past, she set in
motion a deadly plan to destroy
their futures.

Available in February!

 Harlequin Books®